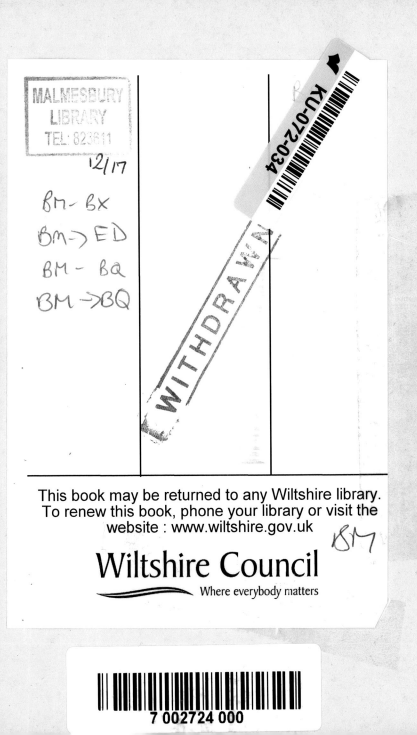

This book may be returned to any Wiltshire library.
To renew this book, phone your library or visit the
website : www.wiltshire.gov.uk

BM

Wiltshire Council

Where everybody matters

Other books in the Unleashed series:

Also by Ali Sparkes:

The Shapeshifter series:

Ali Sparkes
UNLEASHED

A LIFE AND DEATH JOB

OXFORD

UNIVERSITY PRESS

OXFORD
UNIVERSITY PRESS

Great Clarendon Street, Oxford OX2 6DP
Oxford University Press is a department of the University of Oxford.
It furthers the University's objective of excellence in research, scholarship,
and education by publishing worldwide in

Oxford   New York

Auckland   Cape Town   Dar es Salaam   Hong Kong   Karachi
Kuala Lumpur   Madrid   Melbourne   Mexico City   Nairobi
New Delhi   Shanghai   Taipei   Toronto

With offices in

Argentina   Austria   Brazil   Chile   Czech Republic   France   Greece
Guatemala   Hungary   Italy   Japan   Poland   Portugal   Singapore
South Korea   Switzerland   Thailand   Turkey   Ukraine   Vietnam

Oxford is a registered trade mark of Oxford University Press
in the UK and in certain other countries

British Library Cataloguing in Publication Data

Data available

ISBN: 978-0-19-273406-8

1 3 5 7 9 10 8 6 4 2

Printed in Great Britain

Paper used in the production of this book is a natural,
recyclable product made from wood grown in sustainable forests.
The manufacturing process conforms to the environmental
regulations of the country of origin.

**For Rosemary Canter,
who changed my life**

With many thanks to Neil White
for his expert advice on
Special Operations rescue tactics.

1

First came the smell. A stink which crept low across the floor in company with a rolling grey mist. It was the smell of the nastiest sumps of the Thames at low tide—the river's halitosis. Fetid and rank and damp.

Lisa put down her cup and eased round slowly on her chair, drawing a shallow breath.

Next came the water. Dark rivulets snaking across the wine-coloured carpet, beading on the fine woven Persian pattern and sinking into the tassels at its edge. Lisa allowed her eyes to travel back up the delta of tiny rivers to their source—bare toes, blackened by silt and puffy in the brackish tidal flow. The girl stood in a luminous blue light. Her nightgown had been white but was now green or brown or grey, depending on where the weed or barnacles clung. It stuck to her thin frame. Her hair hung in clumps across her face. Once it had been golden and as fine as silk, a perfect frame for her blue eyes. Now it was a dull shade of sludge and the eyes it framed today were washed out and cloudy, like those of a dead fish.

The girl held out her hands, and two frayed bracelets of rope swung on her wrists, heavy with water, silt, and algae. She fixed her dead-fish eyes on Lisa and opened her mouth, allowing a small torrent of dark liquid to escape down her chin before she spoke.

'Left. Abandoned. I was left . . . ' she whispered. Her voice was so heavy with woe it could barely make it out of her throat. 'Left to drown . . . '

Lisa stared at the girl, tilting her head to one side as if trying to understand.

'Left to drown before . . . '

'Yeah, I know,' butted in Lisa. 'Before you were fourteen. Bad luck. But, listen, sister, any chance you could hurry it along today? Only I've got to get going.'

The apparition looked confused.

'Look—it's not that I'm unsympathetic or anything, but I've heard it all three times now,' said

2

Lisa, getting up, pulling her blonde hair into a ponytail and checking her reflection in the mirror. She was wearing new jeans and a funky little yellow top. She looked good if she did say so herself. And she did. Behind her the apparition was still dripping and holding out its hands—but had at least stopped wittering on about not getting to be fourteen.

'Trust me,' said Lisa, sitting back down to tug on her high-heeled Jimmy Choo zip-up ankle boots. 'Being fourteen is no great shakes. Not much different from thirteen. You're better off out of it.'

'I was *left* . . . ' the girl began again.

'Yep. That was a bit of a bummer, no mistake,' agreed Lisa. 'But there's no use dwelling on it, is there?'

She zipped up the second boot, jumped up, grabbed her Fendi satchel bag and left the room, closing the door abruptly on the damp spirit. A few steps down the thick runner carpet of the hotel corridor she turned and rapped on the next door along, ignoring the average looking man who had come out of the room opposite, like a trapdoor spider on a mission. On the third knock the door was opened by a tall, slender girl with dark hair and startlingly violet eyes.

'That was quick,' said Mia, raising an impressed eyebrow and beckoning her best friend in. 'You normally take ages getting ready!'

'I'm not done yet,' said Lisa, stalking into Mia's room and depositing her bag on her dressing table. 'I thought I'd finish up in here with you. We can chat!' She smiled brightly and foraged around in the bag for her lip gloss.

Mia folded her arms and gave a hard stare. 'What is it?' she asked.

'Does there have to be a special reason to want to get ready in your room?' trilled Lisa.

Mia sniffed. She wrinkled her nose and looked around. 'Pshwww!' she commented. 'Is that you?'

Lisa stared into the mirror and rolled her eyes. 'Nope. Not me,' she muttered, through gritted teeth. '*Her.*'

Mia looked around with a shiver. She was highly sensitive but rarely saw what Lisa saw, unless she made an effort. She walked across to her friend and rested a warm hand on her shoulder. At once she spotted the girl walking through the wall. Mia let out a shaky breath. She would never get used to this.

Lisa turned round to glare directly at the spirit.

'BO, girlfriend,' she said. 'You're always the last to know.'

'Lisa!' Mia was shocked. Her friend's rudeness to the dead was another thing she could never get used to. 'She can't help it! She looks as if she was drowned.'

'*Left*,' began the girl, as a fresh tide of water travelled across Mia's floor. '*Abandoned.*'

'I *told* Chambers—*please*, I said. Let us have a *new* hotel!' Lisa stood up and flung her little pot of Molton Brown lip gloss back into her bag. 'No *old* ones! Nothing with any *history*. So where does he put us? An eighteenth century building! Honestly, it's like having to bunk up in a dormitory with three hundred years' worth of gone-off relatives.'

'*Abandoned!*' insisted the girl.

'Why don't you help her?' asked Mia, still holding on to Lisa's shoulder so she could see the spirit, her face crumpling with sympathy. 'She can't be older than us. Poor thing! Look what happened to her!'

Lisa slapped Mia's fingers off her shoulder and, turning her back on the spirit, rested her hands on her hips. 'I don't like to *encourage* them! You *know* that!'

'Yes, I know . . . but couldn't you just—?'

'I am MEANT to be on HOLIDAY!' shouted Lisa, turning back to face the spirit.

It had gone.

Lisa punched the air. 'Re*sult*!'

Mia shook her head and turned to get her jacket from the bed. She didn't say anything but Lisa knew she'd upset her friend. It made her feel guilty. And that made her feel furious. It was not *fair*. She was meant to be having a break. She'd had to wait months and months for this treat—a week-long trip to London—and getting Mia out with her had been almost impossible. Dad had pulled every string available to him and even offered to pay for the extra security detail—and even then it had taken months of wrangling and promises and planning.

And throughout that time, like a good girl, back at the college she had dealt with the dead pretty much non-stop, like a Post Office counter clerk with no relief staff. Without complaint. Well . . . maybe a bit of complaint, but hey, she wasn't a saint.

Mia was brushing her hair now, sharing the mirror. She was dressed in dark green—a close-fitting top and combat trousers ending in shiny black boots with square two inch heels. Her jacket was black and boyish and she pushed the sleeves up to her elbows. It was a tough look. The woven leather bracelet on her left wrist added to it, with its gleam of misshapen black obsidian. But as tough as Mia dressed, the wellspring of warmth from within her softened every carefully planned edge. Mia was a healer. She couldn't help it. Being around her made people feel so good they were apt to stare and even follow. Everyone fell in love with her. It eased off a little after some time in Mia's presence but there was no denying it was damned annoying in the early stages. Lisa reminded herself of this as she planned their next move out of the building. *The choker.* The young porter in reception was so besotted with Mia he literally dribbled whenever they were in close proximity and he was on duty today.

'Wear your choker,' she suggested, as Mia put down her hairbrush. 'In case we bump into bellhop boy!' she added. 'He can't take any more Mia Effect today. He'll be running up and down the corridor and licking the walls soon—and then he'll have to be arrested.'

Mia allowed herself a rueful smile as she dug out

her choker. It was also made of fine black leather strands, woven together with smaller beads of black obsidian and tourmaline. It was pretty but, more to the point, it was useful. While Mia would never give up her strengthening black obsidian, she had agreed to tourmaline as well and this helped to block her effect on people, just a bit. On a crowded street, at speed, sometimes people didn't look at all. And sometimes they were just looking at Lisa. Lisa was worth a look or two—and well aware of it.

'You're good for my ego, you know that?' said Lisa as she clipped her bag shut and shrugged it over one shoulder.

'Can't think why,' said Mia. 'I think you're horrible. That poor girl.'

'No—I mean, good at stopping it running away with itself. I get a lot of attention,' she gave herself a final mirror check, before smiling smugly, 'and so I should after all the work I put in. But you can go out looking like a soldier and you still get all the love.'

'Rubbish,' said Mia. 'You know it's not real.' She looked embarrassed. '*You're* the babe. Who was the one who got approached by a model scout in Covent Garden yesterday?'

Lisa allowed herself a little pout of pleasure as they stepped outside, and allowed the door to clunk shut. 'I want you to mention that, in passing, next time we see Gideon,' she grinned.

'No. You're smug enough,' laughed Mia. 'And don't think I've forgiven you, yet, for being so nasty to that poor drowned girl.'

Lisa sighed as they headed for the lifts and the man with nondescript hair and an unremarkable jacket began to follow. 'Mia—what do you think I can do?'

'Send her on to the next dimension!' said Mia. 'Give her some peace.'

'Ah, yes. That would be great. Waft a bit of incense around and tell her to run to the light, yeah?' Lisa pressed the amber button for the ground floor.

'Yes! Why not? You were given this gift to use it!'

Lisa fought back the surge of anger that rose in her as the lift arrived. *Gift.* Yeah. Right. 'It's not as simple as that. She's a VS.'

'A what?' Mia blinked.

'A VS—vengeance seeker,' sighed Lisa. 'She doesn't *want* to run into the light, she wants payback. She wants to tell me who left her to drown and see that they get what's coming to them.'

'Oh,' said Mia, holding the lift door open for the man with forgettable features. 'How do you know? Did she ask for vengeance?'

'Nope. Never got to it. So far I've managed to get out of there or just confuse or annoy her enough until her energy runs out and she has to wait for the next time. I was hoping she was a monthly one or at least a weekly, but no, she's a daily. Must be *really* narked.'

'So . . . vengeance,' murmured Mia. She smiled at the man. She always felt a bit sorry for them. Lisa didn't. Lisa made a point of absolutely ignoring them.

'Yes—vengeance. Which would involve days if not *weeks* of research, trying to find the descendants of whoever did for her and then trying to get them to understand and then maybe do some kind of séance and all say sorry or maybe just kick over a headstone or something. I don't know. I haven't got time for it. She'll just have to wait for the next poor gullible medium who shows up. I'm not on duty.'

'Oh,' said Mia, again.

Lisa knew Mia only partly understood. Almost everyone in the world thought that being a psychic medium was a strange, mystic, spiritual thing. Something wondrous and thrilling. Well, it bloody well wasn't. Not when you had it *every day*. Right now, for example, as the lift opened to let a middle-aged lady in, Lisa could see an elderly man knocking at the wall with a small hammer. He was knocking and knocking and there was a look of horrific joy on his gaunt face. He turned to look at her and pointed the hammer at her with a knowing, gap-toothed grin just as the lift doors slid shut. And in that instant the reason for his hammering slid into her mind like a cold metal blade. She blocked it fast, but it stayed with her for a few seconds. Murder. It was usually to do with murder. She ejected it before the detail could emerge. How about the lobby, eh? What treat would await her there? The lift opened onto a golden atrium of Italian marble, crystal chandeliers, glistening mullioned windows, an elaborate fountain in a round pool—all overlaid with the perfume of extreme wealth.

A small boy and a smaller girl ran past the fountain, giggling. They glanced over at Lisa as they went, their pale thin faces dappled with death-light and a smell of . . . hmmm . . . yep, that would be cholera. She smiled tightly back at them and shook her head. *Not me. Not today.* Hanged maid dangling to the left of the staircase? Check. Pining Dalmatian dog fading in and out next to the fountain? Check. Indistinct blurry mauve thing wafting about by the concierge's desk? Check. Some kind of footman or butler walking across from the front door to the basement steps—only sunk to his knees in the marble floor (it had obviously been raised in the past century)? Check. Yep. The regulars were all there. Permanently anchored to this place by some trauma or another. Every day Lisa saw oblivious guests and staff wander past, under, and often *through* these apparitions. She carefully sidestepped them and tried hard not to make eye contact.

Of course, there were the voices too. The voices in her head. As soon as she let her shutter up even a little they burst through, a raging torrent of departed souls desperate to get a message back to the living. When this had begun, three years ago, she had nearly gone mad. Back then she had clung to the hope that it might one day stop. It had not stopped. If anything it was worse—but—and this was a crucial but—she had been taught to protect herself. Taught how to put psychic shutters up to keep them out for a while. That was the best gift the

Cola Project had given her. So although she usually still saw everything, she *could* shut off the noise for periods of time. And she had become almost immune to the more shocking visions. Almost.

'Hi, Jeff,' said Mia, as a second man arrived next to Gary, the first one. Jeff nodded and smiled very slightly. It was not his job to like the assets, but who could fail to like Mia?

'OK—Itchy and Scratchy are in place,' muttered Lisa as they reached the huge revolving door which led on to Sloane Street. 'Does that mean we can go shopping?'

Mia laughed. 'Shall we go into lingerie again? I just love their faces when we do that.'

'All the SAS training in the world can't prepare them for frilly bras,' sniggered Lisa.

'Poor men!' Mia glanced back at them across the opulent reception hall. She would never admit it to Lisa, but she was glad to have their constant companions from MI5. She and Lisa, together with around a hundred other Children Of Limitless Ability—or Colas—were listed as the UK's most precious living assets. And as two of the True Eleven—the eleven most powerful of them all—it was astonishing they had been let out at all from their secluded college in the Lake District. Terrible things could happen to Colas. She and Lisa already knew this.

Their minders always walked a discreet distance behind and rarely talked to them—although they would chat to other people at the drop of a hat; they had a remarkable talent for it. At any time at all, if they needed to, they could morph into all kinds of people, from leaflet touts to football fans to concerned dog owners seeking a missing Labrador. Anything and everything to help them blend in. They were under cover and very good at it. They wore clothes which ensured they would not stand out. They were average to look at. They could slip and slide and merge into near invisibility in a crowded London street. They were like wraiths. Because although the two people they were tailing were well aware of them, it was important that it was not obvious to the casual observer that these two teenage girls were anything extraordinary. That they needed twenty-four hour protection, like it or not.

And like it, Lisa did *not*. She constantly had to suppress the urge to shake them off. Only the memory of some of the more awful things which had happened to unprotected Colas in the past three years made her behave and tolerate the minders.

As they waited for the next segment of revolving door to open to them Lisa cast her eyes around the hotel foyer. And then her heart gave a thud and she let out a rare gasp of shock.

'What?' said Mia.

Lisa stared at Mia, her dark blue eyes wide and confused.

'The regulars!' she whispered. 'They've all gone.'

2

Mia took Lisa's arm and hefted her into the next revolving door segment. As they shuffled round to the outside world and the smells and sounds of Sloane Street in summer assaulted their senses, she checked her friend's face. It was unusually pale.

'Are you all right, miss?' asked the doorman, bending stiffly towards them in his long red coat. 'You look like you've seen a ghost!'

Lisa snorted. 'That's just it,' she snapped. 'I have seen *no ghosts at all*!'

'Can I get you ladies a taxi?' smiled the doorman, remembering his job.

'No—we're walking today,' smiled Mia, trying to make up, as ever, for Lisa's rudeness. 'Thank you anyway.' The doorman smiled fondly at her and tried to work out why she somehow reminded him

16

of all his children and grandchildren.

Lisa strode off, flicking back her ponytail and staring ahead. Behind them the minders moved along amid the agog tourists and stony-faced native Londoners, carefully low key but always ready.

'What's going on?' asked Mia. 'Why are you all freaked out?'

Lisa shivered. 'All the regulars—they were there when we came out of the lift and when I looked back they were all gone.'

'Regulars? Oh—you mean the ghosts?' Mia began to puff a little, trying to keep in step. 'Slow down a bit. You'll break your ankle in those stupid boots and then I'll have to mend it for you.'

'These boots are not stupid,' hissed Lisa. 'They are Jimmy Choos! Anyone with a teaspoon of fashion sense would kill for a pair.'

'So . . . the regulars?'

'Yes. All gone.'

'But . . . isn't that kind of what ghosts do? You know . . . disappear.' Mia sent waves of calming healing out with her words because Lisa was getting into one of her moods. The healing just smacked against the girl's shutters, though. It was too late to help.

'They never all snap away at once. The ghost power grid doesn't blow a fuse,' muttered Lisa. 'They fade and they do it in their own time. They don't work together like a West End chorus line, you know.'

'O-K . . . So, maybe they just faded quickly while you weren't looking.'

'No. They didn't. They all went at once. There were six of them there and then they were all gone.'

'So—ask Sylv.'

'I'm trying. But she's not there!'

For the first time Mia heard a sliver of panic in Lisa's voice. She grabbed her friend's shoulder and forced her towards a shop window. 'Stop.' Mia scanned Lisa's face and saw that it was rigid. 'I know what's happening here.'

'What?' said Lisa, through gritted teeth. But her anger was all fear. Mia could feel it thrumming across the short distance between them.

'It's not going to happen again,' said Mia. 'You know that. All the tracker chips are in our clothes and shoes. There's nothing inside your head. Nothing is shutting you down. You're just panicking.'

Lisa opened her mouth to retaliate with a cutting comment, but then she closed it again and let her eyes drop to the gum-freckled grey pavement.

'It is like that, though—a bit. I mean—it reminds me.'

'I know,' said Mia. 'It was horrible. But we were OK in the end, weren't we?'

Lisa's mouth puckered a little. 'Only after Dax dug them out of our heads. It hurt so damn much.' A vision of Dax, shapeshifted to a falcon and driving his vicious curved beak into the base of Mia's skull flared through her mind. The government—the people who were meant to be looking after them—had put tracker chips into them while they were drugged and unconscious. Just as a *safety* precaution, *of course*, to be sure they were never lost. But the tracker chips had been sabotaged to be capable of blocking their Cola powers—and even to explode inside their heads, executing them at the press of a button. Dax had known and he had saved them but Lisa could never forget the horror of having no contact at all with Sylv, her spirit guide, for a few awful hours. Blocked. Helpless. As much as she resented even *having* a spirit guide, she had felt horribly vulnerable without her connection to Sylv.

'Take a deep breath and try again,' said Mia.

Lisa did so and a few seconds later her face

19

softened with relief. 'It's OK. She's back. She says *she* did it. She was trying to get through and I wasn't paying attention.'

'*No!*' Mia raised an ironic eyebrow.

'So she cut out all the other channels for a second.' *That was really not funny, Sylv!* she added, in her head.

I know, came the response. *But I don't have the ability to materialize and kick your backside, do I?*

I've been trying to have a HOLIDAY! Lisa seethed back. *What's so important that you have to freak me out, you heartless ghoul!*

Ungrateful little madam! muttered the spirit guide, and a distinctly earthy choice of words followed, concluding in *I don't know why I bother with you.*

Why do you? asked Lisa. *I never asked you to.*

Oh. Shall I go then? Shall I not bother?

Back on Sloane Street, Mia was watching her friend closely. Lisa's face was awash with reactions to the internal conversation she was having. Now Mia saw her bite her lip and cast her eyes heavenward with a short huff.

No! Don't go. All right! I'm sorry, Sylv. I know you're only doing what's best for me. Lisa kicked the ledge at the foot of the shop window like a toddler caught out fibbing. *What do you have to tell me?*

Hang on—let me check, came back Sylv and Lisa had one of her rare glimpses of the woman who had died ten years ago, when she was only 53. Fair haired, busty, in a blue top and a grey scarf, a cigarette in one manicured hand, flicking through bits of paper on a shiny table somewhere in the realm of the passed over. Sylv had had no children but was a much loved auntie when she ended her time on earth. Lisa often felt that Sylv regarded her as one of her nieces. *Ooh—here it is. Nastier.*

Lisa waited a beat and then sent: *Nastier? Nastier than what?*

I don't know! came back Sylv. *All I know is that you MUST have this word. It's some kind of warning or clue or something. Nastier.*

Well, great! Lisa stepped away from the wall and began to walk again, Mia at her side, trying to read her expression, and the minders moving fluidly not far behind. *Nastier! Well, we don't know what, when, how, why or who—but we can rest assured—it will be **nastier**. Thanks a bunch, Sylv. I'm looking forward to it already.*

Sorry, replied Sylv, and she did sound a bit embarrassed. *When it came through it seemed really, really important. That's why I crashed your holiday. But maybe*

I was wrong. I won't bother you again unless it's a life and death job. Ha ha! See what I did there? Life and death?

'Oh—hilarious!' said Lisa, out loud, but she felt better. Sylv might be immortal but she didn't claim to be perfect. Sometimes she passed plain nonsense on. Her most important role was, in fact, to hold off some of the worse spirits trying to make contact; the kind that didn't care how much a medium suffered. Sylv was her protector more than anything. She'd taken no prisoners in life and certainly took none in death.

'What is?' asked Mia.

'Oh—nothing. Some dumb message from the beyond, again,' sighed Lisa, rubbing her left shoulder to encourage some warmth back into it. Despite the late May sun, the muscles ached with cold. It was a strange physical side effect which she experienced whenever she was in communication with the spirit world.

Mia smiled, brushed Lisa's hand away and replaced it with her own, sending in a quick wave of healing heat.

'Thanks, Mia,' smiled Lisa, at last relaxing. She jumped a little, though, when her mobile phone went off. She dug it out of her satchel. 'Dax,' she said, clicking to speaker mode so Mia could hear. 'Missing us already?'

'Just wondering what London looks like these days,' came back a warm voice. Lisa smiled. Along with Mia and her father, Dax was probably the person she trusted most in the world; her dark-haired, dark-eyed friend at college who was only a part-time human.

'London is sunny, full of tourists, packed with shiny expensive stuff I'm planning to buy,' said Lisa. 'And—most importantly—absolutely free from all trace of Gideon!'

An aggrieved shout in the background told Lisa that Dax had them on speaker too. Gideon was listening in. 'Oi—you brat!' yelled Gideon and Lisa could picture him, all green eyes, and messy blond hair, jumping up off his seat in aggravation. 'Admit it! You miss me like crazy! You're wishing I was there!'

'We wish you both were,' laughed Mia. 'I'll make Lisa buy you some posh chocolate, Gid. And what shall we get for you, Dax?'

'Ah, surprise me,' came back Dax's voice and Lisa wondered whether he had already been out flying around the Cumbrian fells that morning. Or running through the woods as a fox—or swimming the lake as an otter. She so envied his Cola gift. She would swap hers for his in a heartbeat if she could . . .

'Get him some sequinned hotpants!' chortled Gideon. 'For the hot disco fox look!'

'Shaddup, Gid.' There was a thud and Lisa knew Dax had just shoved his best friend over the back of the sofa. A few *doofs* followed. Gideon was undoubtedly hurling cushions at Dax's head, using his telekinetic power. There was only one phone the Colas could use, and it was in public, in the common room of Fenton Lodge. She guessed they were in there on their own though, for Gideon to be making the hotpants gag at Dax's expense.

The line began to crackle. 'Gideon!' she shouted. 'You're messing up the line. Stop teleing!'

'Got to go anyway,' said Dax, panting a little from their exertions. *Are you OK, though?* he sent. *Got a funny feeling, just now* . . . Dax was not fully telepathic, but when they were already connected by phone, or just in each other's company, he and Lisa could talk with their minds. It was to do with his animal abilities. It was much stronger when he was a fox.

I'm fine, she sent back. *Nothing to worry about.*

Aloud, she said, 'OK, we're not wasting precious holiday time talking to you two any more. We've got some serious shopping to do. Byeeee.'

Their friends shouted back a cheerful farewell; a 'take care' (Dax) and an elongated fart noise (Gideon) and were gone. Lisa grinned at the phone, her mood lifted, and put it back in her bag. 'Come on now,' she said, linking her arm with Mia's. 'Let's shop!'

'Are you sure you're OK to shop?' checked Mia, falling into step with her along the busy street. 'After that spirit thing with Sylv?'

Lisa raised an eyebrow. 'No spirit, however nasty, is getting between me and Harvey Nicks.'

Stacey Volkova stepped out of the limousine with her gold Chanel bag slung over her left shoulder and Tolstoy safely in her right armpit. The transparent perspex heels of her Dolce & Gabbana sandals clicked agreeably on the warm London pavement and passers-by paused to glance at her as she sashayed across to the store, doing her super-model walk.

Of course, it was only a matter of time before she *was* a supermodel, Stacey knew this. She could have been on the cover of *Vogue* already if her father hadn't kicked up about her being only 15. A small scowl of frustration flitted across her features, lending a temporary wrinkle to her perfectly proportioned nose and a brief pout to her pink-glossed lips. But that was OK, because she intended to pout. A lot. She'd had some filler injected into her lips last week (Dad would flip if he ever found out) and although it had hurt like hell, the effect was amazing. She looked like Angelina Jolie. Only younger and prettier, of course. This was evident every time she glanced into the high polished windows of Harvey Nichols—which she did a lot, puckering her mouth repeatedly. Well, she'd paid for a fabulous pout and she was determined to use it.

'Rrrrrr,' commented Tolstoy, from under her arm, his dark fur splayed sweetly against the fuchsia pink silk of her strappy Stella McCartney sun dress.

'It's all right, baby,' cooed Stacey, glancing back at Kris and Edwina as they hurried along behind her, ready to both carry her shopping and/or die for her if necessary (well—that's what they were paid for). 'They'll let Tolstoy in, won't they?' she checked.

'Well,' said Edwina, a meaty, mousey-haired woman in her thirties who dressed like a personal trainer but could kill a man with just her thumbs. 'It does say guide dogs only on the sign. Ordinary dogs may not be allowed. He might have to wait in the car.'

'Tolstoy,' breathed Stacey, awash with emotion, 'is *not* an ordinary dog! He is my best friend in the world and was a Prussian prince in a previous life!' Tolstoy growled again, his pinched features dwarfed by huge liquid brown eyes and large point-ed ears. He broke wind delicately. 'I can't leave him in the car, like a suitcase!' insisted Stacey, looking as if she'd been asked to have him shot and stuffed.

'Well, you tell that to the doorman, sweetie,' drawled Kris, a muscular Scotsman in a suit which concealed a dizzying array of weaponry. He looked as if he didn't care, but Stacey knew he would do as she wanted and 'have a word' with the store. Dad-dy was a best friend of the owner, after all. In fact, weren't he and the owner out somewhere with the Prime Minister tonight?

Sure enough, three minutes later, Stacey was trot-ting through *Parfumerie*, Tolstoy still safely tucked under her bare arm, his little paws occasionally walking in the air in memory of how his ancestors used to get about. She moved around the glistening counters, drenched in essence of wealth, like a high-heeled bee foraging for nectar. 'Hello—oh hello! How are you? Hello!' she trilled, almost non-stop, to the sales assistants who stepped forward and beamed at her as if she was a cherished friend. Of course, many of them knew who she was. She was a regular visitor. She'd also been featured in *OK* magazine only last month, pictured at the wedding of a minor royal, wildly outshining the bride.

Stacey prodded and stroked and sniffed daintily at all the perfumes and potions on display. A blonde girl with quite nice Jimmy Choo boots on was spraying something in the air. Stacey sniffed again and then decided to make the girl's day.

'That's lovely. Gift wrap it and put it on my account, will you?' she smiled and turned to move on to the next counter.

'Um . . . pardon?' said the girl—in a rather ungracious way, thought Stacey, in the circumstances. She'd probably just scored a huge wad of commission for the sale.

Stacey glanced back. 'I'll take it,' she said, with a curt nod. 'The biggest bottle you have. You can gift-wrap it for me. My people will take care of the payment.' She waved her hand towards Kris and Edwina and went to glide on.

And then there was—yes, there really *was*—a snort of laughter behind her. She spun round and stared at the blonde girl, who was staring right back at her, one eyebrow raised, an incredulous look on her face.

'Well, thanks, contessa,' said the girl. 'But thrilled as I *would* be to gift-wrap some overpriced deodorant for a random stranger, I'm really not good with ribbon. Maybe you should try asking a *member of staff*!'

'Well, I'm *so* sorry,' said Stacey, summoning up her most superior smile, 'but something about you made me think you *were* a member of staff. Yes,' she looked the girl up and down with a pitying expression, ' . . . you've a definite look of "shop girl chic" about you.'

Lisa tilted her head forward, as if she was addressing a toddler. 'If I *were* a shop girl, I certainly *would* try to get you to buy *this*,' she said, waving the tester bottle of perfume. 'It's made of washing-up liquid, pig sweat, and cat's pee, of course, but you have a definite look of "brainless heiress chic" about you.' She slicked a tight smile across her face and turned to an approaching member of staff, who was looking aghast at the confrontation. 'Oh—good— you're here! I think this young lady needs some advice on hair removal. She seems to have some significant growth in her left armpit.'

Stacey squealed with shock and indignation. 'How dare you?' she breathed. 'This is a long-haired Tibetinan Schizuana! An incredibly rare breed! Worth more than your whole house costs!'

Lisa smirked. 'I doubt that,' she said, picturing the Devon mansion in its rolling green acres.

'And in a former life,' said Stacey, her voice dropping with reverence and awe, 'he was a *Prussian prince*!' She narrowed her eyes.

Lisa's jaw dropped in mock amazement.

The girl simply stood there, open mouthed, *glowering* at her.

'Come *on*,' said Mia, appearing from behind the organic glycerin soap display. 'Enough of the rich bitch stand off. You're attracting attention.'

Lisa snapped her jaw shut again. 'Actually, he *was* a Prussian prince!' She blinked, with genuine surprise. 'Must've reigned *really badly* to reincarnate in your armpit,' she added, as her foe continued to glower at her. She grabbed some free hair removal cream samples from a nearby stand, snorting with amusement, and pressed them into the girl's hand. 'That should get rid of most of it,' she sniggered.

'*Lisa!* Come *on*!' Mia grabbed her friend's arm, shrugging at their minders who were watching closely a short distance behind this other girl's minders. 'Back *away* from the bolshy princess, you bolshy princess.' Lisa allowed herself to be led away, still smirking over her shoulder at the stupid heiress who was now plucking the canine accessory out of her armpit and comforting it with baby talk. Not that the dog cared either way—a more bored creature Lisa had never had the opportunity to mind-read.

'Admit it,' laughed Mia as they headed up the escalator to the shoe department. 'You loved every minute of that. Makes such a change to have someone as rich and snooty as you to have a crack at.'

Lisa shrugged and smiled. 'Well—you're way too nice all the time. And way too poor. And the ghosts are so . . . insubstantial. Yes—a nice hissy fit with a worthy adversary can do me good, I admit it.'

'So—she's not actually stupid after all?' Mia peered at Lisa, amused. '*You* bothered to get into her head!' Lisa could mind-read too, as well as dowse for lost things but she rarely used any of her powers unless provoked or coaxed.

'No, she's intelligent enough, just dumbed down with Daddy's money. Anyway—who cares? Look! Shooooooooes!'

Mia shook her head in wonder, but made no comment about how much 'Daddy's money' Lisa was clearly just about to spend. It would probably outstrip their hotel bill.

Stacey Volkova strode away furiously, her heels striking the marble tiles like ice picks. She stopped a few steps from a metal bin, realizing she was still holding the free hair removal samples which that *odious* blonde girl had put in her hand. With a deft flick of the wrist she sent them right into the bin with one accurate thud and then strode on. Kris and Edwina moved after her silently but she could *feel* that Kris was laughing at her. He'd like to see her taken down a peg or two, wouldn't he? If only because she had made him carry Tolstoy. Oh yes. Maybe Edwina hated her too, but she had a face like a slab of beef—she never gave anything away.

Stacey halted and took a deep breath. She stretched out her long fingers, manicured to perfection, and let the breath out, sending all the negativity with it. She was beautiful. And nice. Everyone who knew her loved her. She must remember this. She repeated this mantra in her mind for a minute, standing alone in the lobby by the lift, deep breathing and pushing away the negativity.

Just as she began to wonder where Edwina and Kris and Tolstoy were, Edwina arrived at her elbow.

'Miss—your personal shopper?' she prompted. 'She's expecting you. You might want to take this lift to Floor Two?'

Ah yes. Stacey smiled. How she wished that jumped-up little blonde could see her *now*, as she went up to meet Simone, her personal shopper, who would guide her to the most expensive collections in the building and treat her like royalty.

'Tolstoy needed a comfort break,' said Edwina. 'Kris is taking him to the nearest lamp-post and catching us up.'

'Good idea, Eddie,' said Stacey. Edwina had never suggested the nickname, but Stacey used it anyway. 'Now, let's go and shop.'

The lift door slid open and Stacey and Edwina

stepped inside and watched the door slide shut again.

'You know—I think I'm going to spend *obscene* amounts today,' said Stacey, just before she lost consciousness.

3

Lisa fell off the low suede stool so suddenly the sales assistant gave a little shriek.

Mia, who had been staring in stunned disbelief at a pair of sequinned flipflops bearing a price tag of £275, spun round in time to see her friend scrambling to her feet, looking dazed.

'You all right?' she said, with an anxious glance around. Lisa's eyes weren't focused on the here and now and that was not a good sign.

The sales assistant laid her hand on Lisa's shoulder before Mia could stop her. Lisa snapped her head round and glared at the poor young woman, who only thirty seconds before had been on her way to making a very good sale, and exhaled in a ragged burst. 'Give it up!' she said, in a hoarse whisper. 'He's not in love with you. He's going to steal from you and bury you in debt.'

'Wha-what?' The sales assistant backed off. She looked freaked out.

'The watch is a fake and he's tried it on with your sister,' added Lisa, her eyes still remote.

Mia grabbed her arm. 'Lisa! Cut it out!' She smiled apologetically at the sales assistant, who was now unlatching a gold-coloured watch on her wrist and staring at it in bewilderment. 'Sorry, she has these turns,' she said.

The sales assistant looked up at her, tears welling in her grey eyes. 'I—I thought my sister was funny last time we saw her. I—I . . . '

Mia stepped across to her, and placed both hands on the young woman's shoulders. Instantly the pain and shock belted through her, along with a bitter backwash of deeper knowledge. This woman, deep inside, was aware her boyfriend was no good.

'You knew, really, didn't you?' she said, sending in waves of healing. The woman nodded, biting her lip. 'You're going to dump him and lock him out today, aren't you?' The woman nodded. 'Good.' Mia gave her a quick confidence boosting hug and then darted across to Lisa. 'Time to go,' she said and steered her friend away from the puddle of ludicrously priced heels and leather.

Glancing back she saw the sales assistant kneel down to sort out the mess. The look on her face was . . . resolved. Good. They'd done some good, Mia told herself, wincing at the cold pinch of someone else's heartbreak inside her. She took a deep breath and tried to get it to dissolve away. It would probably take an hour or more. Emotional pain often took longer.

'Are you feeling better?' she checked, tugging Lisa into the safety of the lift.

'Nastier,' said Lisa, sagging against the patterned silver wall panel as the door slid shut.

'Well, you've been quite nasty enough already today,' said Mia. 'I think we should go back to the hotel.'

'Nastier. Here,' said Lisa.

'Did you eat your breakfast?' Mia touched Lisa's arm again. 'No. You didn't. You're doing your low blood sugar thing again. For heaven's sake, Lees! You should know better by now. You know if you don't eat anything it's easier for the spirit world to wipe out your energy. Ugh! I sound like your *mother*!' Mia clicked her teeth and narrowed her eyes at her angular reflection in the silver panel. No matter how hard she tried to look tough and edgy, the softness just leaked out of her.

'We're getting you a bun,' she said, suddenly stabbing at the buttons by the door.

'*Lift going up,*' intoned a woman's voice. The café, sushi bar and food hall occupied the fifth floor. They could either grab something fast in the food hall or sit down and get something in the café.

'*Fifth floor,*' the lift informed them. '*Doors opening.*'

'*Obscene* amounts,' muttered Lisa. 'What—*you?*'

'OK! Sugar. Coming up.' Mia steered Lisa out of the lift and across to the food hall. Ignoring the price tag, she grabbed a packet of organic chocolate brownies and hurried across to the till. The food hall was quiet, although something else was happening over in the café area, judging by some uproarious laughter and a ripple of applause. Mia put down a note for the brownies while Lisa hummed an odd little tune behind her, beads of sweat starting to glitter on her face.

'Another £2.50 please,' said the man on the till.

Mia stopped herself gasping out loud and dug out the extra. Two minutes later she was feeding Lisa chocolate brownie by the dried pasta shelves. 'Come on,' she said, feeling more like a mother than ever. 'Eat up! Or I'll have to heal you and you know what that's like for me. I'm already heart-broken, thanks to you!'

Lisa jolted and made an effort. It would only be a matter of seconds for Mia to sort her out. They both knew this. But what each had discovered, a long time ago, was that helping people you loved always cost more for any Cola. As soon as Lisa was back on form from Mia's healing, Mia would drop—and drop harder—although she would do her best to hide it. As good as she had become at protecting herself and swiftly getting rid of the pain, grief, and exhaustion she removed and absorbed from others, she would never be immune when it came to the people she cared about. Her friends knew this too. Lisa opened her eyes properly, grabbed the brownie and shoved it in before Mia could start to heal her.

'OK—OK,' she mumbled through brown crumbs. 'I'm good.'

'So what happened?' asked Mia. 'What brought that on?'

Lisa shook her head and screwed up her face, trying to remember. It was like chasing a dream. 'What did I say?'

'Well, you destroyed that poor saleswoman's morning by telling her about her no-good boyfriend.'

'Ah yes,' said Lisa. 'But that wasn't it.' She shivered. Whatever spirit had broken into her shopping fun had to be a pretty powerful one to get past Sylv today.

Mia was looking closely at her. 'You said *nastier* again, in the lift.'

'Did I?' Lisa looked clueless.

'And something about *obscene amounts*.'

Lisa pulled a compact mirror out of her bag and checked her teeth for evidence of chocolate brownie. 'I can't remember it now,' she said, with a shrug. 'Don't worry about it. If it's urgent, it'll come back.' She quickly reapplied her lip gloss while Mia rolled her eyes.

'What's all that racket about?' Lisa stalked off towards the source of the noise. Mia sighed and followed. They found there was a crowd of forty or more people—mostly women—clustered around a young man who appeared to be holding court in the restaurant. Part of it had been sectioned off and the tables re-arranged and there was a sign which read

**'Here today—Mystic Michael O'Flanagan.
Get your signed copy of *Through My Eyes*!'**

She and Mia exchanged glances. 'Mystic Michael?' spluttered Lisa. 'This I *have* to see.' Pushing into the crowd, they worked their way towards the front, where the young man was holding court. He was charming the audience with a lopsided smile, hazel brown eyes, and unruly dark hair that hung around his face in curls which should have been girly, but somehow weren't. He was wearing a pair of dark grey jeans, pointed brown leather boots, a dark grey shirt, and an olive green velvet waistcoat. He was perched on the edge of the table. Behind him were piles of hardback books and an anxious looking girl with a phone and a camera.

'I'm getting . . . P. Someone whose name begins with P . . . ' said Mystic Michael, in a southern Irish accent, lifting his left hand and wafting his fingers through the air.

There was an excited hubbub and one woman shouted, 'My name's Pat. Is it me?' She gazed at him, hopefully, clutching his book to her large chest.

Mystic Michael fixed his gaze upon Pat. Then he pressed his fingertips to his temples and closed his eyes. 'P—Pat? Yes, it could be you. Does the name John or Jim mean anything to you?'

Pat gasped and then frowned. 'Um . . . '

'Or it could be Jean . . . Jenny, even?'

Pat gasped again. 'Jean! Yes—I know a Jean.'

'Aah—Jean. Yes, that's it,' said Michael. 'And is this Jean passed over?'

'Well . . . no . . . I mean, I don't think so . . . ' said Pat, beginning to look rather worried. 'I haven't seen her since we worked at Sainsbury's a few years back . . . '

'Ah no, wait, so,' said Mystic Michael. 'It's not Jean—it's Jean's grandmother. She wants to get a message through.'

'Oh—OK,' said Pat.

'She says Jean was very fond of you when you worked together. She's sending me . . . an image of . . . numbers . . . lots of numbers.'

Pat nodded enthusiastically. 'Well, we were always counting stuff. We worked in the stock-checking department . . . or on the tills.'

'And . . . I'm seeing orange too. Really glaring orange.'

Pat laughed. 'We both went out once, and we showed up in exactly the same top. And it was bright orange. We called ourselves the Tango Twins. Wow . . . that's *amazing*. And her grandmother knows about that?'

'Apparently so,' grinned Mystic Mike. 'Pat, Jean's grandmother wants to say that you should get back in touch with Jean. She says Jean's been feeling a bit down recently and it'll really cheer her up. She says you've had a rough ride of it too in the past year . . . '

Pat gulped and nodded. 'It's true!' she whispered. 'So true! But where will I find her?'

Mystic Michael's handsome features twitched and he pressed his fingers to his temples again. 'I'm sorry, Pat . . . she's fading. But . . . um . . . I think she said "Try Facebook".'

There was a warm chuckle from the crowd which hid the loud snort of derision from Lisa.

'You see,' smiled Mystic Mike, 'even the passed on know all about the internet! Not so very different to what I'm doing now. Just call me the hereafter's search engine. Now, have we got time for any more, Michelle?'

The anxious looking girl behind him snapped her phone shut and said, 'I think only one more, Mike—and then we have to get to the signing!'

'OK, so—let me see.' He closed his eyes and tilted his face up to the zigzag perspex ceiling which folded above them, allowing diffused daylight to touch on his features. 'I'm getting . . . someone with fair hair.'

Lisa's hand shot up. 'That'll be me,' she said loudly, before anyone else could get in.

'Lisa!' hissed Mia. 'You'll get us in trouble!' She glanced around anxiously for their minders—and then realized that their minders were nowhere in sight. The last time she'd seen them was . . . when? Before they'd got on the escalator up to the shoes department. She felt a stab of concern but then remembered that she and Lisa were wearing about eight tracker chips between them. The minders would be around, watching, keeping an eye on their tracer gadgets. They always knew where their 'assets' were.

Mystic Mike was smiling at Lisa. 'OK—maybe,' he said. 'I'm getting . . . Liz or Lisa?'

Lisa giggled. 'Yes! That's me! That's my name—Lisa!'

He smiled some more, making direct eye contact. 'I'm hearing from . . . a . . . woman. Fair haired also. Someone very close to you who has passed into the realm of the beyond.'

'Could it be . . . ' gasped Lisa . . . 'could it be my nan? Carol?'

'She's not giving me her name . . . ' said Mystic Michael. 'But she is related to you. She says you must make sure you eat enough—and not to worry about money.'

'Oh—that's am*azing*!' said Lisa, her eyes wide. 'I'm always worrying about money and I never eat enough! Ooh—by the way, y*our* nan says you've to stop being such an eejit and to lay off all that blarney. You're a bit of an Irish stereotype, so you are!'

There was a shocked pause and then Mystic Michael let out a shout of laughter. 'That—Lisa—was good! Very good accent. Ladies and gentlemen—another medium in the making, don't you think?' The crowd applauded although some of the women shot Lisa disapproving stares.

Mia dug her in the ribs. 'What are you *doing*?' she hissed.

'Oh, he's such a fake!' grinned Lisa. 'I can't believe they're falling for it. I *have* to get his book.'

The medium had sat down at the table now and his Public Relations girl was getting the audience into a queue to have their books signed before being guided to the till. Lisa barged into the queue, ignoring the tuts of the people behind while Mia hung back, feeling edgy. Where *were* Jeff and Gary?

Lisa reached the front of the queue within five minutes. The man was signing his book—*Through My Eyes: the story of my journey as a medium*—with a speedy flourish, twinkling up at each purchaser and exchanging a few words. When Lisa arrived he paused, his pen in his left hand, and smiled at her. 'Come to try me again, have you, Lisa?' he said, with that lopsided grin. His right hand moved to tug at his shirt collar and he looked suddenly vulnerable.

Lisa put down her book. 'No. I wouldn't want to anger the spirits now, would I?' Something in the dark blue of her return gaze made Mystic Michael lose his composure slightly, but only for a second.

'Are you always this . . . challenging?' he said, cocking his head as he opened the book. He was younger than he appeared from a distance. Maybe only 20, she thought.

'Challenging? Ha! This is nothing. I'm usually much nastier than *this*—just ask her.' Lisa glanced across at Mia, who was looking around very edgily. 'But, Mystic Mike, don't *you* find there's only so much you can take of spirits wittering in your ear day and night?'

'It's a gift,' he said, signing in green ink. 'A blessing. Why would I complain?'

Lisa smirked as she collected her book. 'No. I don't think you have *any* reason to complain, Mystic Mike. Roger the Dodger says hi by the way. He says to watch that ankle.'

This time it worked. The man's face went very still. Satisfied, Lisa walked to the till. When she had paid for the book she glanced back and saw that he was signing again. But he'd stopped that mad lopsided grinning business.

'What did you do?' asked Mia.

'Nothing.'

'What did you *do*?'

'Just said hello from his dead college mate, that's all. You'd think it would be no surprise, seeing as he *must* have been chatting to him regularly anyway—on his hotline to the hereafter.'

'You're horrible.'

'Yeah,' laughed Lisa. 'Um . . . by the way, where are Itchy and Scratchy?'

'That's what I've been wondering,' said Mia.

4

Her father was speaking to her. In Russian. 'Wake up! Wake up, princess. Time to wake up.'

Stacey took a sudden, choking breath and shot upright, her heart hammering in her chest. Her hair was hanging in her face, damp and hot.

'Calm down! Don't get in a state.'

No, it wasn't her father—it was Edwina, her body-guard.

'What happened?' she mumbled, wiping dribble off her chin in disgust. She couldn't see very well. Things looked a bit blurry.

'You had a turn, miss,' said Edwina. Her bedside manner was a little lacking, thought Stacey, considering the wage she was on. 'Just take it easy. You'll be fine.'

'Where am I?' She could feel a thin mattress or

perhaps a couch underneath her. It smelt old. Mildewy. This was all wrong. 'What's going *on?*'

Someone else spoke then—a man, but nobody she recognized. 'You may as well tell her,' he said, in Russian.

'I can't be doing with it right now,' said Edwina. 'Have you heard the way she screams? Like a cat in a fat fryer.' Stacey was shocked. If her father *knew* how rude his employee was being . . .

Edwina leaned over and pressed something cottony against her face. Stacey protested. She was quite capable of blowing her own nose. She was . . . was quite . . . was . . .

'You can't knock her out like that every time she wakes up,' said Sergei. 'You'll kill her if you overdo it.'

Edwina shrugged. 'What did you do with Kris?' she said, fiddling with some black and silver gadgetry stolen from the CIA earlier that month.

'He'll be in the ground in less than an hour. Along with the dog.'

Edwina gave a short sigh. 'Shame. A good operative, Kris. But he would never be persuaded to turn.

Ridiculous, old-fashioned patriot. And the other two?'

Sergei smiled tightly. 'In the basement. Your new toy worked brilliantly.'

Edwina allowed a wolfish grin to escape across her thin mouth as she held up the small black box with its short aerial and silver buttons. 'A hand-held EMP!' she marvelled. 'What will they think of next? One little electro-magnetic pulse, directable and measured to the metre! I *am* impressed by our American friends. They make *such* good gadgets for us to steal. How much power did it knock out?'

'The escalator and all the tills and the credit card readers on about a third of the ground floor,' smirked Sergei. 'There'll be a few stiff letters to American Express and Mastercard today, I expect.'

'So what effect did it have on Stacey's extra minders?'

'Both dropped in their tracks,' laughed Sergei. 'And then our own very special first aiders took them to the basement.'

'So . . . ' Edwina peered at the device in her hands with a look of love and awe. 'Did it kill them? Having a little EMP explosion in their earpiece?'

'No. But they won't be waking up any time soon.

And when they do, all their tracers are toast. No way of tracking their asset. So no reports back to Daddy.'

'Better if they don't wake up at all.' Edwina slapped the device back down on the small table. 'I am still surprised. I had no idea that Daddy was paying for extra minders. Ex MI5 by the look of them. What does it mean? Why today? Doesn't he trust me? I have been so loyal to him for so many years.'

Sergei sniggered, but then his pale, thin face turned serious. 'Well, if you hadn't spotted them spotting us, our plans would be in ruins now.'

'Well, I know a spook when I see one,' said Edwina, checking to see if Stacey still had a pulse. 'After all these years I could virtually *smell* them—even in the perfume department. Honestly! *Four* of us for one spoilt brat. The man's paranoid.' She dropped the girl's arm and went back to the portable EMP device again. She picked it up, shaking her head. 'I only brought this along to create a disturbance, to be sure store security would be occupied when we took Daddy's little girl. *Great* good fortune. Nothing else would have dropped an ex MI5 operative in his tracks so neatly.'

'This,' said Sergei, placing his hand on Edwina's shoulder, 'is meant to be. Today, the people of Britain will understand how serious we are. For Radachnya!'

'Take your hand off my shoulder,' said Edwina. 'And save your pathetic speeches for your fellow Radachnyans.'

'Do you have no love for your *own* country?' questioned Sergei, wisely stepping back.

'I love a country—fiercely,' said Edwina. 'The country that pays the most.'

'They've gone,' said Mia. 'I haven't seen them for half an hour.'

Lisa shrugged, but she was worried too. 'Probably just in deep cover. Maybe they're testing us— seeing if we behave. Don't know what they think we're likely to do. Run amok in the food hall and spit in the caviar?'

'Dowse for them,' said Mia, leading her friend into a corner near the lift where she wouldn't be seen if she went a bit trancey.

Lisa sighed. 'I don't have anything that belongs to them,' she grumbled.

'No—but you know their names and what they look like,' said Mia. 'That ought to be enough.'

'I normally have something they've touched,' said Lisa. 'Or a relative. They haven't touched anything anywhere near us—have they?'

'I don't know. Maybe they touched the tracker chips before they got sewn in our clothes,' suggested Mia. 'Stop complaining and just try. This is important!'

Lisa huffed and closed her eyes. After a few seconds she opened them again. 'They're still in the building,' she said. 'I told you—they're just hiding from us.' She pressed the down button to summon the lift.

Mia looked around. She wanted to believe Lisa but something felt wrong. 'Don't you feel . . . ?' She shook her head.

'Look,' said Lisa, leading Mia into the lift. 'We go outside the store. Trust me—they'll be on our trail in seconds as soon as we hit Sloane Street. And anyway—don't you kind of *like* it? Isn't it great that we might be really on our own?'

Mia said nothing. She wasn't fooled and Lisa knew it. The last time they'd been really on their own was when they'd been sold out by a trusted government servant. And they'd very nearly all paid for that with slavery or death. Possibly both. Lisa guessed she should let Sylv in on her thoughts. *What's up Sylv?* she asked, deep within her head.

Don't know, love, said Sylv. *Something's going on . . . but I'm not sure it's anything to do with you two. I'm not picking up anything new from anyone here. Just the same as before. You know—'nastier'.*

Haven't I been nasty enough today? sent back Lisa. *I've upset a princess, a saleswoman **and** a fake Irish medium. Also temporarily broken Mia's heart.*

It's not a bloody competition, you horrible girl, said Sylv. *It was a message—not an instruction. Uh-oh. Look sharp—the lights are out.*

The lift door opened and Lisa and Mia gasped. The usual bright glitz of the ground floor *parfumerie* was now darkness with just a few dim orange emergency back-up lamps and some agitated staff scurrying about.

'What's going on?' Lisa stepped out of the lift and caught hold of a young man racing past with a fluorescent vest on.

'Power's gone out in this section, miss,' he said, turning to her immediately. 'We might have to close the store. Best head for that end!' He pointed a silent walkie-talkie towards the far side of the store, by the jewellery, where the light and power seemed to be normal. Shoppers and staff were congregating there, looking back into the dim area with bemusement.

'Whoa! Maybe it's a heist!' said Lisa, her eyes sparkling, as they headed for the light.

'Well, they picked the wrong department to cut the power on,' observed Mia. 'Jewellery's over the other side. Maybe they were trying for the jewellery bit but snipped the wrong wire.'

'Come on—let's go,' said Lisa as they reached the nearest properly lit exit. 'Itchy and Scratchy will be freaking out in here.'

'Since when did you ever see them freak out at anything?' said Mia, looking around again for their minders. Still no sign. Her anxiety was hard to ignore but Lisa tried hard to ignore it anyway. She hated feeling nervous. She would rather call it excitement.

Outside the light was brilliant and the heat of the day hit them after the air conditioning in the building. They both let out a long breath as they walked along the pavement, feeling relief at the normality. By the time they reached the corner the minders would definitely be back in their slipstream. At the corner a hand fell on Lisa's shoulder. 'You found us, then?' she smirked, turning round to raise an eyebrow at Jeff or Gary. The eyebrow froze. It wasn't either of them.

'Wait,' said Mystic Michael. 'I have to talk to you. They're going to get nastier.'

5

Lisa and Mia looked at each other, then all around them, and then back at each other.

'That proves it,' said Mia. 'I *told* you they were gone.'

Lisa nodded and swallowed hard. 'Yup,' she said, glancing at the man, who was looking agitated and perplexed. 'Itchy and Scratchy would have had Mystic Mary here rolling in the gutter half a street away.'

'Um—excuse me!' Mystic Michael was looking slightly affronted now. 'Did you not hear me? I need to talk to you. It's urgent!'

Lisa got a powerful bolt of adrenalin. 'Taxi!' she yelled as a black cab approached with its For Hire light on. It slowed and she grabbed Mia's arm and pulled her friend towards it.

'Look—have I just turned invisible?' Michael looked amazed that two teenage girls were ignoring him. He was not used to being ignored by women of any age. But then he let out a yelp of surprise as the blonde one turned back and grabbed his arm too.

'In!' she said. 'Get in and we'll talk.'

'Where to?' asked the cabbie, muted by the glass that separated him from his fares.

'Um . . . can you just give us a bit of a sight-see?' asked Lisa as the Irishman flopped into the seat beside her and stared around in bewilderment. The cabbie looked sceptical in his rear-view mirror, so she waved a couple of twenties to reassure him. The cab pulled away into the slow traffic.

Mia was buckling herself into the little fold-down seat opposite. She was keeping herself remote, as she always did when they met someone new, especially someone male and new, but their fellow passenger was already beginning to stare at her. Lisa sighed. She loved Mia and she knew Mia couldn't help it but the 'falling in love' thing did get a bit wearisome.

She clicked her manicured fingers in front of his face. 'Over here. Oooover here.' He pulled his fascinated gaze away from Mia and refocused on Lisa. 'Long story short,' said Lisa. 'Mia's a healer. An amazingly brilliant healer. She makes everyone feel warm and fuzzy. It's why you've just fallen in love with her. It'll wear off a bit soon, but for now, can you just do me a favour and stop dribbling? I can't tell you how much it bashes my ego. I mean— *look* at me!'

Michael did. And then the wonky smile was back. Lisa was something to behold, after all. Long, blonde hair in a perky ponytail, eyes the colour of the Irish sea in summer, a sulky but humorous mouth and pearly skin. Way too young for him, of course, but . . .

'So—now that we've got that straight, what are you trying to achieve?' demanded Lisa, smirking very slightly.

For a moment he just looked at her, as if he'd forgotten why he'd chased her along a London pavement. Then he frowned and closed his eyes, raking his fingers through his carefully tousled dark hair. Lisa twitched. She'd seen him do it for the audience—it was a carefully rehearsed affecta-tion of 'talking to the spirits'. Irritation welled up in her, temporarily dislodging the gnawing anxiety about what had happened to their minders.

'Oh get over yourself,' she said. 'You said—' she affected an Irish accent, delivered with much dramatic panting, '*They're going . . . to get . . . nastier!* So what's that about?'

He opened his eyes and then narrowed them, looking perplexed again. 'Lisa—isn't it?'

She gave him a supercharged smile. 'You *remembered*!'

'Lisa—do you know who I *am*?' He sat back in the deep leather seat, grabbing the hand rail as the cab turned a sharp corner and ran an amber light. He pointed to his face, shrugged, shook his head, raised his eyebrows, undid a button on his brown needlecord jacket. Waited.

'Errm . . . I would guess you're a guy called Mike, trying to flog a book about talking with the dead, mostly to gullible laydeees,' smiled Lisa.

'So . . . you don't watch *The T Show*?' He grinned more now, tilting his head and working the long-lashed hazel-brown eyes to the max.

'Um. No. What's *The T Show*?'

He laughed out loud then, clapping his hands on his knees and shaking his head some more.

'It's a TV show,' said Mia. 'I saw it in our hotel

last night. Goes out at tea time after the news. This guy's the regular psychic medium on it. He's quite well known.'

'Ooooh! So you're FAMOUS!' Lisa took an exaggerated breath of awe. 'Which—apart from the fact I've never heard of you—is *so* impressive.'

'Is she always like this?' he asked Mia.

Mia laughed: 'Yes. You've caught her on a particularly bolshy day, but generally . . . yeah. She's a brat.'

'Look—it doesn't matter.' He let the charm drop and his face became serious. 'I don't exactly know why I'm here. I just . . . got this message. *They're going to get nastier.* And then there was a strong connection with you, Lisa. I can't explain it. I just had to duck out of the signing, shake off Michelle and catch up with you.'

'So . . . nothing to do with me freaking you out because I'm a *real* medium, then?' asked Lisa.

'Look, I'm real!' He looked stung. 'You don't think I could land a prime-time TV slot twice a week just on blarney and lucky guesses, do you?'

Lisa snorted. 'That's exactly what I think.'

'And why should I believe *you're* the real deal, if it comes to that? Anyone who's read my book will know my mate died at college and we used to call him Roger the Dodger.'

'Would they know about your bad ankle?' asked Lisa. 'The one you broke in rugby practice, which has never really healed properly?'

He sucked air in through his teeth and glared at her. 'You could find that out.'

'And I would bother to find that out . . . be-cause . . . ?'

'My fans get a bit tricky sometimes, you know. To get attention,' he said with a patronizing smile. 'They like to stand out in some way, and pretend-ing they don't know who I am is one way. Pretend-ing they're psychic too is another. What can I say? Sometimes I have this effect on girls.'

Lisa made retching noises. 'Mia, get me a bucket.'

'Oh stop it,' said Mia. 'You're turning into Gideon.'

Lisa leaned across the leather seat and took hold of Michael's left hand. It felt warm and quite leath-ery for a young man's hand, as if he'd worked on the land. She squeezed it hard and got a belt of in-formation on him. A torrent of images and sounds and words gushed into her head and assorted emo-tions flung themselves around inside her rib cage. It was a little like emotional white-water rafting.

'You're twenty-one but you pretend to be older, your mother's called Marian and your dad is George and you have a little sister who gave you a silver chain when you left Waterford for London and she's got a dog called Jackie and Jackie isn't too well at the moment, she needs to get him to a vet, and when you were fourteen you fell in love with a girl call Siobhan and she turned you down for a slow dance at the disco and made you want to cry but instead you thumped your best mate because she *did* dance with him and you love curry and you hate sushi and you sometimes have migraines so bad you think you may have a tumour but you haven't so stop worrying and oh—yes— you do have a *bit* of psychic ability and you've your granny Matty to thank for that, she's very proud of you but thinks you ham it up too much and no—I *don't* fancy you.'

Michael was staring at her with a faint sheen of sweat on his upper lip when she finally let go of his hand.

'Are you OK?' said Mia. She shot Lisa a reproachful look and then rested her hand on his arm. He gulped and blinked a few times and then smiled gratefully at Mia as the healing calmed him.

'All right,' he said, looking at Lisa. 'You've convinced me. And now you know—I'm *not* a fake.'

'No, not a *complete* fake,' said Lisa and the smirk had left her voice. In truth, the reading had left her a little shaky too. And she'd lied about the last bit. 'But let's not get carried away. You've got a *bit* of psychic ability and even less medium ability—but you've made it stretch a long way.'

'So—he's got some of what you've got,' said Mia. 'Give him a break.'

'About one or two stars,' said Lisa, with a shrug, staring out of the window at the tourists and the scenery.

'And you're five stars, of course,' smiled Mia, marvelling at the ego.

'Seven,' said Lisa. 'Off the scale, really.'

'And barely registering for modesty.' Mia laughed out loud. 'But now that we've all proved how amazing we are, can we try to work out what's going on? We've lost Jeff and Gary and now Mystic Mike has shown up in a panic. Don't you think the two are connected?'

'Who are Jeff and Gary?' asked Michael.

'Our minders,' said Mia. She looked at Lisa and Lisa read her thought. *Is it safe to tell him anything?*

'Go ahead,' she said. 'He won't tell. I've got *far* too much information on *him*.' She gave him a mean smile and he winced.

'Well,' said Mia. 'We live at a special college for people with . . . unusual talents.'

'What—like a holistic retreat?' asked Michael.

'Ye-ess,' said Mia, suppressing a smile. 'A . . . holistic retreat. Anyway. We don't leave it much. We were only allowed to have a little holiday in London on the condition that our minders were there at all times. But we've lost them. We lost them in Harvey Nichols. If they were still around you'd no way be in this cab with us, famous or not.'

'It all started in Harvey Nicks,' muttered Michael, frowning. 'Even before you two showed up, Sean was telling me they were going to get nastier.'

'Nastier. That's the word I've been getting too. From Sylv,' said Lisa.

Mia sighed. 'Sean—Michael's spirit guide. Meet Sylv, Lisa's spirit guide. Play nicely, you two.' Lisa and Michael both looked slightly self-conscious.

'So it must be about her!' said Michael.

'Who?' said Lisa.

'Nastier.'

'What do you mean?' Lisa frowned. 'Someone

who's already nasty—that we both happen to know—and about to get nastier? It doesn't make any sense to *me*.'

'Well, *there's* a surprise, Seven Stars,' he chortled. 'You've got it *wrong*. It's not *nastier* as in "more nasty". It's Nastya. It's a *name*.'

'Nastya?' echoed Mia. 'That's . . . Russian, isn't it?'

'Yes,' said Michael. 'Short for Anastasia. An old family name. Although she doesn't usually use it. She usually calls herself Stacey. Only her dad calls her Nastya.'

'She? Who's she?' asked Lisa.

Michael looked thoughtful and worried. 'Stacey Volkova. One of my regular clients. I do private sessions. I see quite a few celebrities.' He smiled, raising one eyebrow. 'I charge a small fortune.'

'Is she a celebrity?' asked Mia.

'Not really—she's more, well, what they call a "socialite"—makes a career out of being seen at parties and red carpet events. Daddy's very rich. I see her maybe once a month. These rich kids; the only time they like to listen to someone else talk is when they're being told all about themselves.'

'So—you think someone is going to get her?' asked Mia. 'Kidnap her or something? And . . . there must be a connection with us, because Lisa got told about Nastya—or Stacey—too, this morning.'

'I guess,' said Michael. He glanced back across at Lisa. 'Any ideas, Seven Stars?'

Lisa wasn't looking at either of them. She was mentally tracing back all connections to Nastya. *Well, Sylv? What do you think?*

Yes, came back Sylv, with a flavour of embarrassment. *It is a girl's name. And he knows her. Obviously you were meant to bump into Prince Charming here. He's dishy, isn't he?*

Dishy? Lisa snorted. *He's far too impressed with himself. But come on—is there anything more?*

Michael's voice cut through, talking to Mia. 'Stacey's nice enough. A bit silly, but not stupid—and not unkind, although madly self-obsessed, as they all are. Actually, I think her dog's more interesting. You know, he used to be a Prussian prince in a previous life. Who'd've thought?'

Lisa clicked back into the taxi. 'We met!' she said, just as Mia said the same.

'She was there,' said Lisa. 'We bumped into her downstairs in the perfume section. She had the dog formerly known as Prussian prince in her armpit. I was quite rude to her,' she concluded.

'No!' said Michael.

'We have to go back.' Lisa banged on the glass and yelled to the cabbie, 'Can you take us back to Harvey Nichols? As fast as you can!' The taxi lurched to the left and they all grabbed a hand hold.

'What will we do when we get back there?' asked Michael.

'Well, I can try to dowse for her,' said Lisa.

'You dowse, too?'

'Oh yeah.'

'Show off.'

'Watch and learn.'

6

'It's here,' said Sergei. 'In the lift. Anton will hold the door. Are you ready?'

'Yes,' said Edwina, sliding her EMP gadget and some weaponry into an innocuous black shoulder bag and the chloroform tub into her pocket. She slung the bag over one shoulder and then leaned across and picked up the girl with barely a breath of effort. Stacey hung limply in her arms, her expensive sandals swinging in the air like baubles.

'Still alive?' asked Sergei.

'She's breathing,' said Edwina.

'You don't care for her at all, do you?' said Sergei, glancing left and right in the dim corridor. 'After all these years.'

'She's a toy. An empty headed dress-up doll. Why should I care about her?'

'Still,' he said, 'maybe we should keep her alive after the video . . . as a back-up plan? In case anything goes wrong and we need money.'

'You keep forgetting,' said Edwina, walking fast and fluidly towards the lift lobby. '*I* am the one getting paid. A lot. *You* are the one who's doing this for your country. Whether she lives or dies is no odds to me. But fair enough, we may as well keep her alive until we're sure it's all gone to plan.' She reached the open service lift where Anton, a short, dark-haired man with badly pock-marked skin, stood waiting in delivery driver overalls and cap, next to a large armoire-style wardrobe.

His eyes widened when he saw the girl. 'Pretty,' he murmured, reaching for the mahogany-and-mother-of-pearl door and pulling it wide.

'Pretty heavy,' grunted Edwina and flung the girl inside while Sergei pulled the metal concertina lift door shut behind them with a sharp rattle.

Stacey landed like a rag doll, but made only a muffled thud as the inside of the wardrobe was thickly lined with bubble-wrap, twelve centimetres deep on every surface. Edwina dug back into her pocket and then wiped the girl's mouth and nose once more with a cotton wool pad soaked in chloroform. 'That should keep her in by-byes land for another two or three hours,' she said, placing the used material back in the plastic tub and snapping the lid shut before climbing inside the wardrobe too. 'I hope you boys have been working out. This is going to be one heavy delivery.'

Anton kept the lift locked and stationary long enough for Sergei to put on a matching delivery driver's uniform and cap. Now transformed into a nondescript working man, Sergei rested his hand on the wardrobe door, ready to shut both females in, but paused as his mobile phone buzzed in his overalls pocket. He scooped it out and flicked it open, his face taut with focus. 'Yes? Yes?' He nodded and let off a volley of Russian. Then he smiled. 'It is all in order,' he concluded. 'We will send the video within the next two hours. And then it is all up to you.' He snapped the phone shut again and nodded at Anton.

'Come on, come on,' said Edwina, like a busy headmistress. 'Harvey Nicks staff to avoid. Teenage heiresses to abduct. Prime Ministers to kill.'

The lift began to move down to the loading bay.

'And the extra bodyguards? Definitely gone?' asked Anton, his eyes narrowed with anxiety.

'Still dead to the world. Put out with the trash,' grinned Sergei. 'They'll be crushed when they find out.'

'We should call Control,' said Mia, as the cab battled through the traffic along Grosvenor Place. 'They may not know we've lost Gary and Jeff yet.'

'Oh come on. They'll have trackers on our trackers on our trackers,' snorted Lisa. 'I bet they're staring at our little red dots moving around the West End like a very boring computer game right now, and betting on how long it takes us to reach Harrods.' She flipped open her mobile phone and saw a missed call. Control. 'See,' she said, showing it to Mia with a sigh. 'Five minutes ago. They're already on our case.'

'But they may have lost contact with Gary and Jeff too,' Mia pointed out. 'And if they haven't, then they'll definitely know we've gone AWOL. Call back.'

'Rubbish signal,' said Lisa, staring at the shaky half a bar of reception indicated on her phone.

'Try mine!' Mia handed her mobile over. It also showed a missed call from Control—and the signal was no better.

'Mike—can we borrow yours?' asked Mia. He handed it over, bemused, but again the reception was too bad, the call resulting only in a succession of high pitched beeps.

'It's him, probably—and me,' said Lisa. 'Too much psychic interference.'

'Well, thank you, Seven Star,' said Mike, tipping an imaginary hat.

'Low grade stuff always makes static,' she said, smartly.

'Look—this could be serious,' said Mia. 'Control will be freaking. Maybe they think we're planning to run off.'

'What, strip naked and barefoot so we can go shopping?' said Lisa.

Michael looked mystified and slightly pink in the face. 'What *are* you two on about?' he murmured.

'There must have been a glitch with the trackers and their gadgets, that's all,' said Lisa. She closed her eyes briefly. 'Sylv isn't sure it's connected with Nasty girl. It's probably just a coincidence. And anyway, if we're going to help Prince Charming here with his mystery kidnapped client, we won't get very far with Itchy and Scratchy back in tow, will we?'

Michael was shaking his head. 'Is she *on* something?' he asked Mia. 'Or has she just been overdoing the Disney channel?'

'They'll find us soon enough,' reasoned Lisa. 'Or Control will send back-up. We'll go back into Harvey Nicks and I'll dowse again—for Nasty girl first—see if we're meant to get involved or not. And when we've found her, if they haven't already found *us*, I'll try again for the minders.'

'OK,' said Mia. 'But if we've not got any answers in twenty minutes, I'm calling Control from a phone box. I don't care what you say.'

'Have your minders *really* got tracker chips on you?' asked Michael, who seemed to be very slowly catching on.

'Yes,' said Mia. 'Loads of them. In all our clothes and shoes. Everything we wear gets chipped and pinned! Well—chipped and sewn anyway. We don't even know where all the chips are. We just have to promise to wear only chippy fashion or else . . . end of holiday.' She shrugged.

'Are you two out on parole or something?' he asked.

'Seems like it,' muttered Lisa. 'OK—here's our stop.'

She paid the cabbie and they piled out onto the pavement, back outside the department store. Michael kept his head down and placed himself between them as they walked across to the nearest entrance. He slid a pair of sunglasses out of his jacket and put them on.

'What's wrong with you?' asked Lisa, giving him an elbow in the arm.

'Just keeping a low profile,' he muttered. 'In case, you know, any fans are about.'

Lisa sniggered. 'Or the paparazzi?'

'It's happened before.'

Inside the store the lights and power were now fully restored and everything appeared normal. Lisa walked to the spot where they had met Stacey/Nastya and stopped. Mia and Michael waited on either side of her, looking around and hoping nobody would pay much attention. Lisa closed her eyes.

'Anything?' asked Michael, taking off his shades.

She opened her eyes and glared at him. 'Give me a chance!' She closed them again and then sighed. 'Nothing. But I don't know her—and I don't have anything that belonged to her; that touched her.'

'I've held her hand,' offered Michael. 'Not for

about three weeks, but I have. I always hold a cli-ent's hand at some point,' he added, defensively, catching a look passing between Lisa and Mia. 'It's what we *do*!'

Lisa took his hand once again and tugged him across to her with a huff. She closed her eyes again. A wave of nausea hit her and she gulped and swayed, vaguely aware of Michael steadying her with his free hand. There was a smell . . . chemical . . . and another, dank . . . mildewy. Then a crackly noise. Then . . . she turned around, spinning slowly like a compass needle while Mia anxiously moved away to distract a looming cosmetics sales assist-ant with a lipstick-related query. 'She's not here,' Lisa said. She let out a long sigh. 'But I'll tell you something . . . ' She felt her mouth pucker with a lightning stab of upset, although what she was feel-ing was just a premonition of someone else's pain. 'Her dog's dead.'

Michael pulled his hand away. 'Are you winding me up?' he said, in a low, unamused voice.

'No,' said Lisa, opening her eyes to meet his. 'I'm not. Dog's dead. Stacey doesn't know yet . . . but she will. I've just got a little sneak preview of that from Sylv. Which is good.'

'Good?' Michael still looked wary and sceptical.

'Yes . . . good,' said Lisa, folding her arms and glaring at him. 'Because she'll have to be *alive* to feel it, I'm guessing . . . Anyway, she's not here, although she *was* until quite recently—just minutes ago. I'm getting a pull to the east. I can follow it, but I've no idea where it'll take me. It's all a bit vague.'

'Are you getting nothing else?'

'Something like motion sickness,' she said, briefly closing her eyes again and swallowing. 'And a crackly sound.'

'Do you think she's travelling somewhere?' he asked.

'Yes, probably. Look—why don't you just phone her mobile?'

Michael rolled his eyes. 'I did that before I came after you. It's on voicemail.'

'So—maybe she's just having an off day and not taking calls,' shrugged Lisa, eyeing the jewellery department glinting across the shop floor and wishing she could just get on with her day. Her *holiday*. 'Look, maybe this is a lot of fuss about nothing. It could even be that she *does* know her dog's dead. Perhaps you were just getting a little premonition about that? I mean—that dog meant a lot to her, so that could be it, yes? A big psychic spike of pain from a valued customer . . . '

'Yes,' he admitted. 'It could. But if so, why has a Seven Stars hotshot like *you* been called in to help? Why not leave it to the Irish amateur, eh? I mean, dead pets are easy. I can channel a forlorn woof at *any* time!'

Lisa pursed her lips and eyed him speculatively. She knew there was something in what he said—after all, Sylv wouldn't bother her with anything so trivial as a dead dog.

Mia came back, having headed off the sales assistant. She noticed a couple of women across in the Dior section staring at Michael and beginning to giggle at each other.

'Come on.' She took Lisa and Michael by the arm and steered them towards the escalators. 'You're getting noticed,' she told him. 'Lees—can you try again for Jeff and Gary?'

Lisa nodded, beginning to feel like a telephone exchange. They paused at the foot of the metal steps, now climbing again in the usual smooth motorized fashion. It was the last place she remembered being aware of their MI5 shadows. She closed her eyes again.

A second later her lids pinged open again. 'They're here now!' she said. 'But . . . they're not . . . their minds are . . . cloudy. Like they're sleeping. Or drunk. And . . . I can hear beeping.'

'Beeping? What . . . like a phone or something?' asked Mia.

'I don't know!' said Lisa. 'Just beep beep beep. You know. Beeping!'

'But where?' asked Mia, clutching her arm. 'Come *on*! They might be hurt!'

'No—just—a little drunk or sleepy,' said Lisa. 'Outside . . . but inside.'

'And you call *me* a chancer!' said Michael. 'What's *that* supposed to mean?'

Lisa collapsed on the floor. Her face turned white and her eyes widened. 'Oh God,' she said, in a voice like gravel. 'My legs—I swear they just snapped in half. They . . . one of them . . . his legs have broken.'

'Now?' Mia dropped to her knees and grabbed Lisa's shoulders. 'Now or soon?'

'I—I . . . ' Lisa's eyelids fluttered.

'Oh no! Don't you faint!' Mia sent in a shock wave of rousing energy and Lisa rallied, her colour returning. 'I'm not picking up their pain through you,' said Mia. 'So it's not yet, is it? It's a premonition! If it was now you know I'd feel it through you. We're not too late to find them and help.'

'Down,' said Lisa. 'They're down below us.'

'Outside and inside. Beeping. It's got to be the loading bays in the basement,' said Michael. He put his sunglasses back on and strode off. 'Follow me.'

Lisa got up, legs fine again and attitude safely back in play. 'Who made him leader?' she muttered.

Michael was walking fast towards two dull grey swing doors, signposted STAFF ONLY. He glanced back at them, grimacing behind his sunglasses, and made 'hurry up' gestures, while looking left and right. The store was fairly busy and no sales assistants were wandering past as they reached him. Of course, any number of CCTV cameras might be in operation, but there was no point in worrying about that now, thought Lisa, as they pushed through the doors. On the far side was a large stairwell, its landing broad enough for lockers and ample passing space for goods trolleys. A sign on the wall showed that they could reach the basement from here. Above them someone was ascending the stairs.

'Well?' said Michael, flicking a concerned glance upwards and then pointing down. 'Are you getting the trail? Is it down here?'

'Yes,' said Lisa, allowing her dowsing brain to take over. 'Follow me.'

She began to get that sense of drunkenness again, tinged with fear. One of them . . . Jeff, she thought . . . was dimly aware of danger but seemed unable to do anything about it. She began to run down the steps, her heart speeding up. All of a sudden she realized that she was maybe the only thing between their faithful MI5 minders and a gruesome, leg-breaking fate. Maybe death. Yes . . . probably death. She felt her insides shrink up tight, as if getting her ready for a punch to the gut. She shivered. She was going to have to be brave, she knew it. She did not want to be a heroine. She had not planned for this at all today. For a start, her heels were way too high . . .

7

Through the smeared perspex upper half of the swing doors, they could see the goods bay, awash with orange strip light and packed with lorries, crates, boxes, wooden pallets, and metal cage trolleys stacked with goods. As they pushed through the doors there was a waft of exhaust, brick, and oil, along with the burble of lorry engines, the bass hum running through the air conditioner ducting, muted voices and sporadic clatters and thuds. Someone had a radio playing loudly in one of the lorry cabs. There was so much noise the three new arrivals didn't need to whisper.

Michael pulled them both behind a stack of boxes, glancing around anxiously. As soon as they were spotted there would be a swift on-the-spot enquiry about what they were doing down here. A dapper young Irishman and two teenage girls were bound to stand out. 'Where are they? Can you dowse through all this?' he asked.

Lisa nodded. 'I know where they are . . . I just don't know how we reach them without getting noticed,' she said.

'Do we care about getting noticed?' asked Mia. 'Surely this is an emergency!'

Lisa opened her mouth to agree, but then clamped it shut again, with a grimace, as the steady *Beep Beep Beep* of her premonition suddenly cut through the cacophony of the loading bay.

'Oh no! The bin! They're in the bin!' she yelled and began to run. The horror in her voice rang out and Michael and Mia shared a glance laden with sudden and awful knowledge. Two semi-conscious men were undoubtedly lying helpless inside the store's industrial sized metal waste bins. And reversing towards them, its filth-encrusted crusher bar limbering up and down in its chamber like a dragon's jaws, was a mammoth non-domestic refuse collection lorry.

Reaching the driver wasn't easy. He was on the far side of the bay and they had to weave through trucks and stacks of goods while the metal prongs of the purpose built refuse lorry were already locking with the first giant skip-like bin, making it judder.

'STOP! STOP!' screamed Lisa and Mia. Michael just sprinted for the driver's cab.

There was no sign of anyone hearing or seeing them. Now the bin was being lifted, its lid being pushed open and flipped back by the loading mechanism on the refuse truck. Lisa felt sick as she recognized a hand, fingers moving feebly, amid a multicoloured pile of rubbish. The men must be buried. No way that the driver would ever see them before . . .

'Oh God!' she moaned, as Michael and Mia bawled 'STOP! STOP! STOP!' at the driver. Michael pounded on the side of the truck as he ran along to the cab. The bin was tipping and an avalanche of rubbish was beginning to cascade into the vast grey mouth of the truck's crushing chamber. A human form began to tumble with it.

Lisa heard herself shriek, like an animal. And the fear she felt was not just her own. It was Jeff's and Gary's—the most awful gut-wrenching horror she had yet experienced through her 'gift'. Death. Awful, painful, horrific unavoidable death—here it came and here she was dowsing it live, right now. *That's me done, then.* That was Jeff. Closing his eyes. Seeing a woman and a little girl. His wife and daughter.

Lisa screamed again, but the howl and crunch from the metal jaws just feet away from her drowned it out. A thud across her head, a brain-spinning impact—saliva—or blood—slewing across her vision. Cold smash on her brow. Air blasting out of her. Screaming . . . Hair ripped. Wrist, snapped, teeth exploding. Gary's last words. *Sweet Jesus, help me . . .* Lisa felt her eyes roll back up into her head and hoped for oblivion. When she hit the floor she didn't feel it.

Men shouting brought her round. Trainers and boots stomped past her face as it lay, squashed and damp, on the concrete.

'Careful! Carefully now!' she heard someone shout. It was Mia. Mia's grown-up, controlled voice. 'Let me get to them. I know—yes, I know—but I'm a trained first aider.'

First aid? Lisa murmured in her head. *Last rites more like. Oh hell, Sylv, is there any way I can get away from this without looking?*

You've no need to worry, said Sylv, sounding kind. *You did well.*

I felt them die, Sylv. How did I do well?

A cool hand rested on her head. 'Hey, Seven Star, stop lazing around.' Michael's face appeared at an angle, pale but smiling, his dark curls flopping sideways.

Lisa sat up slowly, allowing her head to catch up with reality. She was covered in sweat and beginning to shiver out the trauma. 'Are . . . are they OK?'

'Yes.' He steadied her shoulder, nodding. 'Another two seconds and they'd've been dog food. We stopped the driver in the nick of time. Your friend's looking after them now. Emergency services on the way.'

Many seconds passed while Lisa just stared at him, her brain a fog and only slowly recovering. She could make out her face, blank and smooth like a blanched bean, hovering in his eyes. She had experienced death so many times—but always as a replay. The spirits that wanted her attention never seemed to tire of graphic re-enactments for her information and delight, no matter how often she asked them to cut it out. And yet there was still something of her which remained apart, a tiny shred of herself which was insulated from the horror. This time, though . . . this time . . .

'I was dowsing death—*live*,' she murmured,

at last. Michael made a sympathetic face but she could tell that he had no idea.

'They didn't die,' he said. 'You saved them!'

'Dowsing . . . takes you around the moment . . . ' she tried to explain. 'A little behind, a little ahead . . . to what might be . . . ' She fixed her eyes, dark with shock, on his, and he gulped. Maybe he got it a little. Maybe. Maybe he didn't deserve to get it. Who did? She looked away.

Mia crossed to them and knelt beside her. 'They're OK,' she said. 'In shock, I think, but not badly hurt. They can't hear very well. I think something happened to their ear-pieces. Nasty hot pain in one ear canal—both of them got the same thing. Hey—are you OK?' She lifted her hand.

'No touch!' said Lisa, flinging her arms up in front of her. 'You do not want this.'

Mia shook her head. 'Come on—I can take it.'

'I don't *want* you to take it. Not this time.'

'OK.' Mia sat back on her heels. 'Ambulance will be here in a minute. And I'm calling Control now.' She took out her mobile phone. No signal at all in the basement. She stood, looking for a landline, and spotted one in a small, glass-walled office nearby. She made for it.

Lisa stood up. 'Who did this to them?' She felt angry and suddenly oddly protective of their minders, now that she knew there *were* still minders left to protect.

Michael rubbed his hands across his face, looking rather sick. 'The same people that have Stacey. We *have* to find her.'

'I guess it's time we told the police,' she said. 'They'll have people swarming around the city in no time if her dad's such a big shot.'

'The police won't have a clue where to look,' he pointed out. 'You do. You said—east. Have you still got a trail on her? Can you still dowse after all this? I would understand if you can't now. I mean . . . I'm pretty freaked out from the last ten minutes, let me tell you. I could really just do with a lie down right now, so I could. Truly—if you can't go on, just say.'

Lisa narrowed her eyes at him. He was playing her and she knew it. But he had no need to. She couldn't ignore Stacey's situation. Sylv wouldn't let her for one thing . . .

Mia came back then. 'I've called in. Control's sending people,' said Mia. 'They were anyway. But they won't let you go anywhere. We'll be in lockdown after this, you know. Major panic mode for Cola Club.'

Lisa glanced around the loading bay. Most of the people in it—drivers and goods porters mostly—were clustered around the back end of the refuse truck where Jeff and Gary had been laid out, wrapped up in blankets, now conscious but barely talking. A wheeled metal cage a few feet away was filled with clothes. She squinted at them, hoping for the best, and then sighed.

'Great,' she muttered. 'Just great. Leisure wear.' She shook her head and bent over to grab hold of her left boot.

Michael looked mystified. 'Is she channelling again or something?' he asked Mia, but Mia shook her head and bit her lip, beginning to giggle in spite of the gravity of their situation.

Lisa handed her Jimmy Choo boots to Mia. 'Do NOT lose these,' she commanded. 'And don't let Mystic Mickey here move from your side.' She took off her ankle socks too, and then stepped away, the concrete cold and very grounding on the soles of her feet. She reached the cage and then slipped inside between the thickly hung racks of clothing, where she shrugged off her designer satchel and then proceeded to remove the rest of her carefully chosen outfit, grumbling at the unfairness of her life. Even the underwear would have to go. She would not put it past Control to organize chips in their bras and pants too. She stripped away everything that could possibly contain trackers, including her earrings and her moonstone bracelet. Then she riffled through the hanging clothes to find something she could bear to wear. Tracksuits. *Fabulous.* Expensive, no doubt—but still, shiny, puffy, awful, middle-aged lady tracksuits. She found some black track bottoms in her size and then a shiny silver sweatshirt with the words FOXY LADY printed down one sleeve. She shuddered her way into them, wondering with a wry flicker of a smile what Dax would make of the top. Then she transferred a roll of £20 notes from her bag into the deep hip pocket. They'd come out of the bank that morning—they couldn't be chipped. She left her credit cards and mobile in her bag, along with her underwear and jewellery. Then, finally, bundling her jeans and top together, she stepped back out of the cage.

'Scrunchy,' said Mia, with a sympathetic smile, as she took the bundle and the bag. Lisa's nostrils flared with annoyance, and her hair tumbled around her silver shoulders as she handed the thick black elastic band to Mia. It was unlikely, but she wouldn't put it past Control to chip that too.

'O-K. Anyone going to explain any time soon why she's just turned into Sporty Spice?' asked Michael, peering at Lisa's new look with wonder.

'While we travel,' snapped Lisa, hearing sirens. 'Mia—cover for me as long as you can. We'll call as soon as we've found Stacey and let the police take over, but don't send them after me. It'll slow us down.'

Mia nodded. 'Take care,' she said.

Nobody paid Lisa and Michael any attention. Of course she knew there was a good chance that later her exploits would show up on security camera (*dear God, there couldn't be one right above that cage, could there?*), but she guessed anyone who would normally be manning the monitors was occupied down in the bay itself—it was teeming with people now—security staff and first aiders. As Mia returned to look after the injured minders, Lisa and Michael hared back up through the staff stairwell and although two women hurried past them, neither paused to question them. They were intent on reaching the drama downstairs.

'What about your feet?' asked Michael, glancing at her bare toes as they arrived back on the sales floor. 'You're never running barefoot through London!'

Lisa headed straight for the escalator and the shoes section. There, the sales assistant she had left heartbroken an hour before was nowhere to be seen, much to her relief. While Michael stood edgily to one side she swiftly tried on and purchased some running shoes, relieved that she had been carrying enough cash. As soon as Control heard she'd gone AWOL they would run checks on her credit cards to see if she'd left a spending trail, so those were not an option.

The sales assistant made no comment when Lisa turned down a bag and just put the running shoes on to her bare feet. They were a good make; her usual brand. As soon as they were laced up she felt a belt of power. She was a runner. With the right footwear, she could run fast, anywhere, for hours if need be. In traffic-choked London she would be the fastest thing on the streets.

But would her new friend be able to keep up? 'Come on,' she said, grabbing his hand and running for the stairs which led down to the street level exit. 'I hope you chose those boots for comfort . . .'

8

It turned out that Mystic Mike *was* quite well known, after all. As they ran along the busy pavements, dodging in and out of clusters of tourists, Lisa heard the occasional gasp and murmur of 'Ooooh—that's Michael O'Flanagan! Off the telly!' and noticed that people were turning round and craning their necks, probably trying to spot a camera crew tailing them. 'He's doing one of those street psychic shows, I expect,' she heard one girl say to another as she held up her mobile phone and tried to video the fleeing celebrity.

'Put your sunglasses on, for pity's sake!' she hissed at him and he fumbled in his jacket pocket and soon had his eyes shaded again. To give him his due, he was keeping up, Lisa had to acknowledge. But then, she wasn't running as fast as she could.

They had to negotiate not just crowds of sightseers but mad cab drivers intent on mowing them down on crossings, persistent leaflet pushers, high-speed bike couriers, and pizza delivery scooters. She could have screamed with frustration. Adrenalin was pushing her to run like the wind . . . but she could only go at the pace of a summer breeze.

'Where are we heading?' puffed Michael, neatly avoiding a dustcart which a street sweeper had abruptly shoved into their path. 'Are you getting anything?'

'I'm getting water—moving water. I think it must be down by the river.'

'How close?' he panted, taking off his jacket as they ran on through the warm afternoon.

'Not sure . . . not very far. Minutes away, I think.' They moved into Lower Sloane Street and here at last she could speed up as the road became leafy and more residential, leaving behind the shoppers and tourists. They swiftly reached another junction and she saw Chelsea Bridge Road stretching away on the far side. She felt an almost physical push towards it. 'Yes—that goes to the Thames embank-ment,' she said, grabbing his arm and pulling him out into a gap in the traffic. They got hooted at by three cab drivers but managed to get to the other side. Another three or four minutes of hard running brought them to Chelsea Bridge. Lisa halted as they reached the tree-lined embankment.

'Well—do we cross the bridge?' puffed Michael, grabbing a railing and leaning over to catch his breath.

Lisa closed her eyes. She felt the tingling push—down to the water. This side of the river . . . to the left of the bridge. She went with it. Glancing left and right and up above them to be sure nobody was paying attention—and happily the embankment was relatively quiet—she wriggled between a gap in the railings and slid quickly into the cover of some shrubs. Michael followed, with some struggle as the gap was a much tighter fit for him.

Lisa ducked down into the cover of the leafy bushes and a few small trees and kept her head low. 'We can be seen from the bridge if we stand up tall,' she called back to Michael in a low voice.

He grunted, scrambling along behind her. 'I just hope your psychic compass is working!'

'It is,' said Lisa. The sensations were getting much stronger. 'She was brought here in a van . . . or maybe even a lorry. No—she *was* in a lorry, inside a big box with someone else. Someone who was . . . controlling her. Then she was transferred to some other vehicle, probably a car . . . bundled up in some kind of material . . . '

'Was she hurt? Scared?' asked Michael.

'No . . . I don't think so. She was . . . annoyed and . . . sleepy.'

'O-K.'

'You care about this girl, then?' asked Lisa, batting a springy branch away from her face and letting it ping back into Michael's as she moved forward.

He spluttered and spat out a leaf. 'Well, I don't know her that well. I've no idea why the spirits got *me* on the case. Probably only to help *you*. I'm just a sidekick to Seven Star today. Normally I'm the main act.'

'But you care enough to duck out of your own book signing and run around London with me?' Lisa peered back over her shoulder, curious.

Michael shrugged. 'Well—of course! Look, my little sister's only a year younger than Stacey. I would hope someone *she* confided in every few weeks would take the trouble to go after *her* if she was kidnapped.'

Lisa paused in her scrambling and stared at him

for a few moments. 'Well,' she said. 'Aren't you the real deal?'

'So are you,' he pointed out. 'You don't even *like* her.'

Lisa grinned. 'If I could avoid helping everyone I didn't *like* my life would be a total holiday. Ah— look. Shhhhh!'

They were close to the water's edge now. The shrubs on the bank gave way to a short muddy slope of no more than a metre which dropped into the gently lapping brown tide of the Thames. A little way along this bank a small motor boat was at anchor in the shadow of Chelsea Bridge, which loomed over them. Lisa tilted her head as she examined the boat.

'Yup,' she said. 'That's it.'

'You think she's on that?' asked Michael, crouching next to her.

They peered at the vessel, which was a dull grey thing, probably white when it was first launched, with a bleached wooden deck and low level wheelhouse. Its grimy windows offered no glimpse inside. Elderly coils of muddy rope lay on the deck and a tidal mark of green algae decorated its stern above the waterline.

'One way to find out,' said Lisa. Without a backward glance she stepped into the water, instantly feeling its cool invasion in her new trainers. She went in immediately up to her knees and Michael reached out for her hand.

'Careful! You don't know how deep it is!' he hissed, looking around anxiously in case they were spotted.

Lisa held on to his hand but gave him a scornful glance. 'I dowsed the bottom first! I'm not an idiot.'

'Even so,' he muttered. 'It could be . . . you know . . . quicksand. And how are we going to climb up—?'

He abandoned his query as Lisa reached across, grabbed the low bow of the motorboat and athletically pulled herself up onto it. The vessel rocked in the shallow water as she clambered onto the deck. Surely anyone on it would know they'd been boarded? A few seconds passed but nobody shouted out or emerged angrily from below. Lisa shrugged and raised her upturned palms to him before pointing at the wheelhouse.

'Are you coming then?' she asked.

Michael put his jacket back on, looked down at his jeans and fine leather boots, bought only last week for his book launch, and sighed. He stepped out into the water.

She was rocking. Stacey felt as if she was on one of the baby rides at the fair. She opened her eyes but saw only dark, dim shapes and beneath her a carpet of tiny diamond lights which winked and danced.

'Pooh,' she muttered. 'Smells here. Ugh.'

Wherever she was, it wasn't comfortable. And her bangles were digging into her wrists, and the side of her face, where her cheek rested against her hand. Ow. Hang on though . . . she hadn't worn her bangles today. She . . .

Stacey sat up and at once the bangles dragged her wrists right down like lead weights. They were so heavy she couldn't get up. And they were actually *clanking*! Clanking?

Stacey! Wake up! These are NOT bangles, you ditzy miss! She forced her eyes to open properly and adjust to the light. As she did so, her other senses began to click back on line. She was alone. Alone in a dark place, crouching on what felt like rough wooden planks. And the metal around her wrists was not, of course, any kind of jewellery. It was heavy metal cuffs attached to heavy metal chains.

'Oh my,' said Stacey, dimly aware that she

sounded a little like Dorothy in the *Wizard of Oz*. *Darkness and smelly and chains—oh my!*

And the winking dancing diamond carpet . . . well, it was all the light she had. And she knew what it was now. Water. All around and beneath her. She was on some kind of floating deck . . . a pontoon. In the dark. Chained. Alone.

Stacey was well brought up and not given to swearing. Somehow, though, *'oh my'* didn't seem quite enough.

Michael joined Lisa on the deck much less gracefully, with a tide mark of muddy brown at thigh level. Lisa sat on the deck, smirking at him. 'Needn't have bothered,' she said. 'She's not here.'

'What? Well, why couldn't you have said that before I got half the Thames in my unmentionables?' He glowered at her.

'Just couldn't resist it,' she sniggered.

'Look, don't you think it's a *little* more important to focus on the task in hand?' he snapped. 'Are you sure Stacey's not here?'

'Go and look,' said Lisa. She had already been below deck, having forced the flimsy lock on the wheelhouse door, but even before she'd done that she knew Stacey wasn't there. 'She *was* here. This was definitely where they put her next. Although they got her on here further along the river—not here, under the bridge. And then they went . . . ' she pointed east, ' . . . that way. She's somewhere dark . . . damp. Can you drive a boat?'

'What—this boat?' He looked bewildered.

'Well—yes! Can you?'

He squinted at the wheelhouse and then went inside to look at the controls. 'Seems simple enough,' he called out to her. '*If* you have the key! It's got an ignition thing like a car. And no—I don't know how to hotwire an engine!'

Lisa rolled her eyes. 'I never thought I'd hear myself say this, but oh, for Clive, right now!'

'Clive?' Michael peered up at her as she crouched in the wheelhouse doorway.

'A science geek and all round engineering genius at my college,' she said. 'No paranormal talents at all, but extremely useful!'

'Look—maybe it's time we called in the police now,' admitted Michael. 'They can come down here in a launch or something and you can guide them to where you think Stacey is.' He took out his mobile phone and flipped it open. 'Damn. *Still* no signal. What is it with that today?'

'Must be the bridge,' said Lisa. 'Big chunk of metal messing it up. Go back up on the bank. I'll stay here.' She grinned.

'Oh yes—very funny! We'll all watch the poor Irishman wallow about like a hippo again, will we?' Michael narrowed his eyes at her as he shoved his phone back into his jacket pocket. 'You're an unkind child, Seven Star.'

'Unkind maybe,' she said. 'Child—not for some time.'

He landed back in the shallows with a splosh and waded to shore. Lisa looked around, her radar out for anyone watching or approaching but really there were too many people in the area. Any one of them could be watching. Filming with their phone—anything. But at least they were in London, city of the pathologically unimpressed. You had to spray yourself in bronze paint, pretend to be a statue and then come to life before anyone would react around here.

Michael reached the bank and struggled back up through the shrubs, his jeans clinging wetly to his shins and ankles and his socks squelching in his ruined boots. He had to get right back up to the road before he could get a signal. He pressed 999 and was just about to hit send, wondering exactly how he would explain this whole bizarre situation to the police, when there was a scream.

'Aaaaaaaaaaaaargh! Look! Look! It's Mystic Michael!'

He gulped. Oh no . . . not *now*! A crowd of young women was bearing down on him, and the squealing and babbling was already getting embarrassingly loud. 'Michael! Michael! Is that really you? Yes, it is him—it *is*! Hey—can I have my photo taken with you? Hey, will you give me your autograph?'

A second later he was enveloped by a dozen over-excited students. It was a situation he was used to and normally handled with great charm and aplomb—but this was seriously bad timing.

'Oh—hello—look, ladies—er . . . yes, hi! Ooh—now less of the touching, there's a good girl! Er . . . look, I'm kind of in an emergency situation here. I really have to call—oh—oh—OK—look, just one big group photo, OK? Then I've really got to—No—really, I can't sign your . . . your . . . arm. No—no pen. Oh—have you . . . ?'

Back on the boat Lisa was unaware of the

commotion on the Embankment. She filtered out the noise of the distant traffic and focused on dowsing Stacey's rapidly cooling trail, trying to leech as much essence of the girl out of the boat as she could. East—yes—but then where? Somewhere . . . dark. With water. So—probably still on the river or close to it. And alive. Yep—Stacey was still alive; Sylv agreed with her on that. It would be good to have something a bit more concrete by the time the police got here, though. Ideally she'd have an actual location by then and could just send the cavalry in without her and get back to the hotel and find Mia. Maybe they'd even get a bit more shopping in before the end of the day. Oh, who was she kidding? Control was going to have them on an armoured coach back to Cumbria fifteen minutes after she got back to the hotel. No question. Dax and Gideon would laugh themselves stupid when they heard about the girly shopping trip gone mental.

Watch out! yelled Sylv. Lisa opened her eyes and glanced around, confused. She felt the boat rock a little. She saw nothing but white cloth. She didn't even have time to cry out before the fumes knocked her senses flat.

9

'Daddy, I'm all right. I haven't been hurt.' The girl on the screen looked pale and scared but she was clearly not going to cry. A shame, thought Sergei as he held the camera steady and gestured for her to continue. It would work better if she did.

'They say you have to do something for them—you'll know what it is when you get this message—and then they'll set me free and I'll see you very soon.' Stacey gulped and battled to keep the wobble out of her voice. She was descended from Russian royalty and she was damn sure she was going to behave like it. Although it was hard to act dignified when you were chained to a wooden pontoon which continually tipped to one side and threatened to dunk you in the water.

The light from the video camera revealed plenty

of detail about her prison which, on balance, she would rather not have seen. Some kind of concrete ceiling hung about a metre above her, dripping with black-green algae, which clung to it in sticky lumps. There were pillars of elderly brick rising out of the water, holding up the ceiling. The space she was floating in was long and narrow, like a tunnel, and the daylight which had lit the water before the camera flare eclipsed it, came in from several metres away, rebounding off a half brick, half concrete wall. Small brown shapes occasionally swam through the water. She tried not to notice.

The man filming her was kneeling above on a narrow wooden walkway which rested on more brick pillars. She guessed this was some kind of secret boatshed or semi-submerged passageway. She hoped not a sewer. But where? How far had she been taken? She had no idea how long she'd been unconscious. The last thing she remembered was waking up with Edwina in some poky little room . . . and then she was here.

'OK—now say, "*Please do as they say, or they'll kill me*",' said the man.

'I think he's going to work that out for himself,' said Stacey, with more hauteur than she would have guessed she could muster. She was very scared. But angry too, and that was keeping her together.

'Say it!' he grunted and she sighed—and said it, trying hard not to look too pathetic.

'What are you going to make him do?' she asked, as the man put down the camera and stared at the display on it. 'Give you money?'

'I do not care about money,' he snorted.

'But he has lots of money,' said Stacey. 'If you let me go I can get money for you. Millions.'

The man stared at her for a few seconds and then spat into the water.

'O . . . K,' said Stacey.

He began to move away, stooped over, using the camera light as a torch and leaving her in shadow.

'Do I . . . have to stay here? Alone?' she called after him, raising her hands with a clank of chains. And now there *was* wobbling in her voice and she couldn't stop it. 'C-couldn't you leave a light? Please . . . ?' As much as what she had seen repulsed her, the dark now seemed so much worse than before.

The man muttered something in Russian. '*Stupid rich bitch*,' it sounded like. She stopped pleading.

She guessed she would be here for many hours before her father gave them what they wanted and she was freed. The prospect of not being freed she would not even entertain. That way lay hysteria. But just thinking of hours here in the wet, smelly dark, with only the swimming and scurrying nameless brown things for company was nearly as bad. She was almost never left alone. She thought of all the people she had seen that day and decided to revisit them all in her mind—to pretend she was just re-tracing her steps. The driver of the car which had taken her out shopping, Kris . . . what had happened to Kris? . . . Edwina . . . who seemed to be involved in this kidnap thing . . . who would have thought it? Who else? The doorman at the store. The girls on the perfume floor—that horrible blonde one who had been so cutting to her over the sales girl mistake. She'd even been nasty to Tolstoy. *OH!*

For the first time, Stacey realized that Tolstoy was not with her. What had happened to him? And for the first time, Stacey allowed herself to cry. She didn't care how royal her blood was. She was having a truly rotten day. She slumped over on the pontoon and then had to grab a corner of it to stop herself sliding off and being left dangling from her wrists, up to her armpits in water. 'HEEEELP!' she shouted. 'SOMEBODY HELP MEEEEEEEEE!'

Her screams thudded dully against the concrete ceiling. She had no idea how far she was from civilization. She could be in the middle of the Atlantic for all she knew.

'PLEEEEEASE!' she howled. 'Don't leave me down here on my own!!!'

There was a flash of light and footsteps on the walkway and suddenly the pontoon was rocking wildly again. More chain clanking and metallic chinks as the light danced about, lighting up another person—two—depositing something on the pontoon next to her.

'Your wish is granted, princess,' said Edwina, with a nasty laugh. 'You've got company. Hey—it'll be a girly sleepover. Too bad there's no pamper packs!' And then she and the man stomped off, muttering to each other, leaving her once again in darkness.

As her eyes grew accustomed to the gloom and once again picked out the distant daylight sprinkling its diamonds across the water, the shape next to her on the pontoon began to take form. It was making her resting place steadier, whatever it was, balancing out her weight. She put a tentative hand out and felt . . . hair. Someone's long hair—soft and well conditioned, like her own.

It was a girl. She was breathing—alive. And now coughing and rolling over. *Trying* to roll over; the heavy metal cuffs were holding her down. There was a long-drawn breath, silence for a few beats . . . and then a sigh.

'Oh *great*,' said the girl. 'Just great.'

'Who are you?' whispered Stacey.

'Well, *fabulous*,' went on the girl. 'Nice to see you again, Stacey. Well . . . actually, I'm lying. It wasn't nice the first time and it's a hell of a lot less nice now.'

'You!' gasped Stacey. 'The nasty girl!'

'Yeah,' said Lisa. 'And you're Nastya.'

By the time he'd escaped the girls and then finally managed to call the police, Michael was feeling hot and jangly. He needed to get back to Lisa, but he had wanted to tell her that help was on the way. And now it was . . . probably.

Telling them who he was had not helped. The woman on the end of the emergency services phone obviously watched *The T Show*, knew Michael O'Flanagan well and thought there was a very real possibility she was being wound up.

'No—really, I *am* Michael O'Flanagan, and I know, at least I think I know, the whereabouts of a kidnapped girl . . . Stacey Volkova. Have you heard about her? Has anyone reported the kidnap yet?'

No, said the woman, after a pause and a check on her computer. They had not. And how, exactly, did he know the whereabouts of a kidnapped girl? And in what way was he involved? And what was his address . . . and his *real* name? And why did he believe the girl had been kidnapped? And how did he know where she was if he wasn't involved? Oh— was it through his psychic powers? Oh really?

In the end he had given them the number of Josie, his agent, so they would call and confirm he was who he said he was before sending any police cars. And then he had to call Josie and try to explain the whole mad story when all she really cared about was finding out why the hell he had cut and run from a lucrative and carefully organized signing session in Harvey Nichols.

'Are you insane, Michael?' shrieked Josie. 'Do you *know* how hard it is to get an event in Harvey Nicks? Michelle is beside herself, trying to find you. She thinks it's all her fault. You left her with a crowd of hormonal women baying for you to come back—and no explanation! What the hell is going on?'

'Josie, please, sweetheart—trust me, this is a genuine emergency!'

'Don't sweetheart *me*! I don't care what emergency you're dealing with—and if you tell me you can't make it to the Sadler's Wells event tonight I am going to scream until your face melts!'

'No—no, I will make it!' he promised, hastily. 'Josie, just listen to me! Before the police call, you have to listen to me. You have to back me up. It's a matter of life and death!'

It was not easy to explain, but at last a call came through on the other line from the police and Josie, ever the professional, was able to confirm that he was who he said he was and yes, he really *did* mean what he was saying and no, he wasn't a crackpot and no, it wasn't a publicity stunt either. So it was getting on for fifteen minutes before Michael made it back down to the boat—only to discover that the boat was gone.

He stared at the place it had been, panic surging through him. There was no sign of it as far as he could peer in either direction along the river. What had happened to Lisa? Why hadn't she called to him? Shouted out? Made telepathic contact, even? In the distance he could hear police car sirens. His insides clenched. Without Lisa he could not tell them where to look for Stacey. All he knew was that his wealthy young client was imprisoned somewhere dark and damp—out east.

He slumped onto the muddy bank, hidden by the shrubs around him, and groaned. This was bad on SO MANY levels. Bad enough that *two* young girls of his acquaintance had now mysteriously disappeared . . . and suspicion was just about to engulf him like an avalanche . . . But even once he'd convinced the police he was innocent and merely being guided by spirits, his reputation as a psychic was going to be well and truly sunk. He'd come to the end of the road. He could not dowse. And he had no idea what to do next. What help could he be?

'LISA!' he shouted. 'LISA!' Just in case she was hiding somewhere, laughing. Maybe she'd just got bored with waiting for him, hotwired the controls of the boat after all and gone on herself? But no . . . no, she was not in the mood to do that. She had wanted to dowse Stacey's location and hand over to the police and have done with it.

'OK—calm. Calm. *Think!*' he told himself. *What*

happened, Sean? he asked. Sean was sometimes there to help; sometimes not. Unhelpfully, his spirit guide was more likely to make contact when Mike was very relaxed and just sweet-talking an audience than in times of great stress and need. Michael knew he would have to get his head straight and his panicky heart to slow down before he'd stand a chance of reaching Sean.

Gone east, he got back, a couple of minutes later. *Two girls. Bracelets of iron. East.*

Michael gulped. *I don't like the sound of 'bracelets of iron'. Why didn't Lisa shout for me?*

No time. Whiteness came and then blackness.

Michael saw Lisa being chloroformed or something, and knew that it wasn't just his imagination. The pins and needles tingle that always came with true sixth sense washed over him. Certainty. That *was* what happened. The sirens were just above him on the bank now—and he could see what looked like a police launch heading swiftly across the river towards him. His agent must have convinced the police that he wasn't pulling a stunt. Thank God for Josie!

The launch swept up beside him, sending a wash of muddy water over his boots. 'Michael

O'Flanagan?' called one of two officers on board the semi-inflatable vessel.

'That's me,' he said stepping out into the water. The officer who wasn't at the helm of the launch radioed through to colleagues at the roadside above them and confirmed that they'd found Michael O'Flanagan and yes, it really *was* the guy off *The T Show*.

'OK, I'm going to take a leap of faith,' said the officer who helped him aboard. 'I know this is probably a load of cobblers, but just because my missus is a fan, suppose you tell me what's on your mind and where we've got to go, eh?'

'East,' said Michael. 'We go east along the river. Fast. Please. I'll tell you the rest as we go.'

As the outboard motor revved and the launch reared across the water he heard himself add, in his head: *What rest? What the hell are you telling them next? Your head is empty! Sean, you've got to give me more! What happened when she was taken? Where is she now?* Nothing came back. Michael knew he was going to have to blag it; go on instinct for a little while until the next genuine chunk of spirit help came through. 'Come on, Mickey boy,' he muttered to himself beneath the thrum of the outboard, as the

officers peered at him both expectantly and scepti-
cally. 'You do this all the time. You know the form.
Just go into your act and hope for a gift from the
dead . . .'

10

'How do you know that name?' The voice that emanated from the dim shape next to Lisa was scared—and very surprised. 'Only my father calls me Nastya.'

'Well, maybe I was calling you "nastier",' said Lisa, even though she knew that being flippant was a bit out of place here and now. 'As in "more nasty than the last time I saw you".'

'You were in the *store!*' said the girl, her voice drenched with astonished revelation. 'You were rude to me.'

'You were rude to *me!*'

'Oh, I think not! I was being very kind. I was thinking you would like some nice commission on that perfume!'

'And *still* with the sales assistant thing!' marvelled Lisa. 'Try to understand—I DON'T WORK THERE.

I was out shopping for *very expensive things.*'

There was a sigh in the darkness and then a stout rejoinder. 'Well, good for you! So was I. Look how well *that* worked out for both of us.'

Lisa laughed, beginning to dislike Nastya slightly less.

'So . . . Nastya . . . what kind of a name is that?'

'It's Russian. A shortened form of Anastasia. I am related to Anastasia Romanova, of the last Russian royal family. Please, call me Stacey. Only my father calls me Nastya.'

Lisa shrugged in the gloom, making the chains on her wrists clink. 'Whatever. Stacey. Although Michael O'Flanagan knows you as Nastya too.'

'Michael?' Stacey tried to sit up and made the little pontoon swing about wildly.

'Steady!' yelled Lisa. 'You're going to tip us over!'

'Sorry.' They stayed still until the swaying settled down. Then Stacey went on, 'Michael? How do you know Michael?'

'Michael is the reason I'm in this mess with you, instead of having a shopping bonanza with my best friend,' muttered Lisa. 'He picked up that you were in trouble and asked for my help in finding you.'

'Asked *you* for help? Why would he ask you? Do you know him?'

'Never met him before today,' said Lisa. 'But he found me anyway—because I'm a psychic medium too. A much better one than he is.'

'But he's amazing,' breathed Stacey, and Lisa didn't need to read her mind to note how much she worshipped the young Irishman. 'He knows just *everything* about me!'

Lisa clicked her tongue in annoyance. 'He does *not*! He's just a chancer—a cabaret act.'

'Well, he's trying to save me!' Stacey argued, hotly. 'Without him I'd still be on my own down here. Without him, you wouldn't be here to rescue me, would you?'

'Ah yes,' said Lisa. 'Remind me to tell him well done! And about that rescuing thing.' She clinked her chains. 'It's not going too well, is it?'

Stacey was silent for a while. 'Was Michael with you when they caught you? Have they got him too? Or did he see you get taken? Maybe he's going to come in and get us out.'

'I was on a boat—one that you were on for a while, probably the one that brought you here. I'd dowsed for you and that was where I was led to.'

119

'Dowsed?' echoed Stacey.

'It's a kind of psychic satnav,' dismissed Lisa. 'Anyway, we'd got as far as the river and knew you were off somewhere to the east, but we couldn't get the boat working without the keys to the engine and Michael had gone back up the Embankment to get a signal on his mobile and call in the police. He was taking an age . . . and the next thing I knew, there was something white being shoved in my face and then I was out like a light. So . . . hopefully he saw that . . . hopefully he's getting help and will find us.'

'Of course he'll find us! He's a psychic like you.'

'Not like me,' said Lisa. 'I told you—he's not very good. I am extremely good. He's . . . average on a good day.'

'That's so mean,' said Stacey. 'Are you always this mean?'

'Yes,' said Lisa.

There was a long pause and then Stacey, with a wobble in her voice, said, 'So . . . extremely good as you are, tell me what happened to Tolstoy.'

Lisa said nothing. She wasn't *that* mean.

'My dog. Tolstoy. He's dead, isn't he?'

'I think we've got other things to worry about

right now,' said Lisa, clinking the chains again.

'I knew it.' There was a smothered sob and Lisa shut herself off as quickly as she could. She could not be dealing with the girl's painful thoughts.

'Look—you have to focus! Why have they taken you? Is it for money?'

'No,' sniffed Stacey. 'He said not—the man who did the video. He said he didn't care about money.'

'Video? They shot a video of you?'

'Yes—to send to my father. To make him do something.'

'Do what?'

'I don't know! He wouldn't tell me.'

'OK—so who is your father? What does he do?'

'He's a diplomat,' said Stacey. 'He's Russian. My mother's English. Although she lives in America now. They're divorced.'

'So . . . your dad meets up with British ministers and the like, while he's doing his diplomat stuff?' Lisa was beginning to get a very bad feeling. *Top dog*, said Sylv, suddenly back in her ear again. *Top dog. Red carpet. Bolshy. Sharp diamond.*

'Yes—all the government ministers know him,' Stacey was saying, with pride in her voice. 'He's very important.'

Top dog, repeated Sylv. *Red carpet. Bolshy. Sharp diamond.*

'Oh, Sylv! Will you *try* to make sense!' huffed Lisa, out loud.

'Erm . . . my name's not Sylv!' said Stacey.

'Not you,' snapped Lisa. 'My spirit guide—Sylv—she's chiming in but she's not making any sense. *As usual!*'

'Spirit guide!' Stacey sounded hugely impressed. 'That's so . . . cool! Michael has one of those. Say hello to her for me!'

Lisa ignored her. *What do you mean?* she asked Sylv, but Sylv just repeated her bizarre string of clues. *Top dog. Red carpet. Bolshy. Sharp diamond.*

'Stacey—Sylv's getting some information to do with your father,' said Lisa. 'Does any of this mean anything to you?' She repeated Sylv's words, adding, 'It doesn't make sense to *me.*'

'Well . . . red carpet,' mused Stacey. 'Daddy's always going to red carpet events. He's got one tonight. And top dog? Well, he mixes with a lot of people who could be called *that*. Or maybe it's about Tolstoy? Is it? Does Sylv know about him?'

'No—it's not him,' cut in Lisa, quickly. 'What about bolshy?'

'Well . . . that's probably *you*,' said Stacey. 'I've never met anyone bolshier!'

'Thank you—but Sylv knows that already. This is something else. Bolshy! Think!'

'Um . . . well . . . could she mean Bol*shoi*? The ballet?' replied Stacey. 'Because I think that's what the red carpet event is tonight, that Daddy was going to. Of course, he probably won't now . . . not once he's got that video of me.' She gulped and Lisa found she was grudgingly impressed at how well the girl was holding herself together. Most girls of her background would be screaming and sobbing and pleading for a cashmere blanket and therapy by now.

'Or maybe he *will*,' said Lisa, as a new thought entered her head. 'Who else is going to the ballet with him?'

'Oh, loads of top dogs!' said Stacey. 'Ministers and celebrities. Models and TV people . . . It's a huge benefit performance of . . . *Swan Lake*, I think . . . for some big international charity thing. Daddy's always going along to things like this, to meet people and press palms. Poor Daddy. He has to shake hands so much he needs to use a special hand cream. Aloe vera and chamomile and tea tree oil.'

'Er . . . OK, if you say so.' Lisa rolled her eyes in the dark. She really needed to keep this airhead focused.

'Oh, it's not because he's being fussy,' Stacey replied quickly, defence in her voice. 'He has psoriasis. It's a skin condition like eczema . . . but it affects his joints too. He can't wear any rings or watches or anything because even pure gold or platinum sets him off with a terrible rash. He says the macho politicians are a nightmare for him, with their firm grip handshakes. He's in such pain with it, but he mustn't let it show.'

'OK—fine—Daddy has hurty hands. I've got it. Now . . . so we think the top dogs may be at the Bolshoi ballet event tonight . . . but what about *sharp diamond*? Does that mean anything?'

'I don't know. I have lots of diamonds, of course…but none that are sharp.' The pontoon rocked as she slumped down onto it. 'I'm tired and hungry and thirsty. Are you going to get us out of here?'

'Me?' Lisa held tight to the wooden platform as it rocked wildly again.

'Haven't you got a plan?'

Lisa sighed. A plan. She always seemed to have

to come up with something in a crisis. Nobody ever rescued *her*. It was extremely unfair. She spent ninety per cent of her waking life (and a fair bit of the sleeping life too) helping out myriads of troubled people—dead and alive—like it or not. It all seemed a bit one way.

She was thirsty too. And this nasty dark backwater stank. And there were rats using it as a spa. And poncey Irish Michael O'Flanagan—him with his annoying hair and eyes and quirky smile—had probably just run back to his book signing and left them to it by now.

What am I going to do, Sylv? she asked.

Sorry, love, came back Sylv. *I need more connections. I am trying!*

What's going to happen? she asked.

Um . . . I don't know yet. Sylv sounded sheepish. *But . . . on the bright side, you don't like the clothes you've got on.*

Meaning? Lisa winced in anticipation.

I think you're going to get wet.

11

'So—now we have *two* teenage brats to manage,' said Edwina. 'Didn't we have this planned down to the last detail? How could this have happened?'

'Maybe it was a coincidence!' said Sergei, pouring a small shot of whisky into his coffee. He leant against the battered sink unit to drink it, as Edwina eyed him with hostility from the other side of the dilapidated boathouse.

Once the home of a long-abandoned tour boat business, the boathouse had been chosen as the perfect location for this stage of their plan. Far from any working security camera network, the access point to the derelict boatshed was obscured by overgrown weeds at the river's edge, and further screened by a broad thicket of unkempt buddleia bushes on the land side. Overrun with rats and choked with floating debris, the channel that led to the underground shed was only just wide enough to admit the launch. They'd had to change boats half a mile away, transferring the wrapped-up unconscious girl from the old wooden motorboat into a sleek, low-level launch under cover of some high unkempt shoreline weeds. The first vessel was later returned to its mooring, in case its neglectful owner happened by and alerted the river police. The plan was to be as low key as possible; to attract no attention.

'It was not a coincidence,' said Edwina. 'It's the same girl she was talking to in the store before we took her. Whoever she is, she was looking for Stacey. She was waiting for help from someone on the bank.'

'And how do you know you weren't seen, knocking her out and driving the boat away?'

'I *don't* know. I had to act fast. I'd anchored the boat and I was waiting for my pick up on the embankment when I looked down and saw her sitting on it! I recognized her straight away and when I used my audio booster I heard her talking to herself! She was muttering about "Nastya"! That's what Stacey's father calls her. Nobody else knows her by that name. The blonde girl must have been put in place by Volkov, to follow his daughter. Another plant we did not know about.'

Sergei shook his head. 'She's just a girl! She can't be more than . . . what? Fifteen? Sixteen maybe . . . ?'

'Or a twenty year old recruited because she looks so young,' said Edwina, picking a clump of river weed off her wet trousers. 'It doesn't matter. We aren't safe here any more. We have to move Daddy's little princess.' She checked her watch. 'We have only four more hours to wait, and then we'll have achieved our aim and none of this will matter. But we have to move to the other location.'

'Two girls!' Sergei clunked his mug of coffee and whisky down on the grimy drainer. 'One is bad enough! How can we move two without getting noticed?'

'We'll only take one,' said Edwina. 'We'll leave the other one here.'

'What . . . to give details to rescuers?'

Edwina raised an eyebrow. 'She won't be giving details to anyone.' She leaned over and pulled up an iron ring in the wooden floor beneath her feet, opening a square trapdoor, through which the gentle sloshing of the dark water could be heard, along with the muted, indistinct words of the two captives.

'Aah. Teenage chats!' She smiled up at Sergei with eyes so flat and cold that even he was chilled. 'Nothing that one broken neck can't cure.'

Michael knotted his fingers in his hair, his forehead in his palms, and tugged hard, as if trying to pull a clue out of his brain. *Come on, Sean! For the love of God, please . . . now is the time when I really need your help. Tell me where they've taken Lisa! Help me! Guide me! Tell me where Stacey is!*

The launch scudded across the river, bumping off the water with surprisingly jarring thuds. Sean sent him the spiritual equivalent of a shrug and a sigh. *I'm trying. Can only see red. A river of red.*

Oh no! Red . . . as in blood? Michael instantly pictured Lisa lying in a Thames backwater, bleeding to death. Was that real? Was it a genuine vision or just a horrifying fantasy? He was awash with pins and needles, but that probably had more to do with panic than prescience. Focus! He had to focus if he was to find Lisa. And Stacey too, of course. But he could not deny that Lisa was his first thought. He had brought her into this and he felt horribly responsible for her now. He reminded himself that she was seven stars to his two. She was much more powerful. Surely she would send out a big telepathic burst of information to her people . . . those 'Control' people she kept talking about.

'Getting anything, Mystic?' said the officer who was not at the helm of the launch. He had been taking messages on his radio about Stacey Volkova and so far nobody had reported her missing. 'Only her father's PA says she's out shopping and perfectly fine.'

Michael lifted his head and stared at the young officer whose face was set so solid and impenetrable. Then . . . oh glory be . . . a little pulse in his chest; a constriction in his throat. Something was coming through.

'They'll never know about the test, Doug,' he said, the words as sure and solid as silver pennies on his tongue.

'What?' The man looked taken aback. His eyes skittered to the left, as their eyes always did when Michael was bang on.

He took care to speak only loud enough for Doug to hear. 'The little lie. In your interview. The one that got you into the river police section.'

Doug stared at him, his grey eyes wide and his

mouth opening once and then closing, heedless of some static chatter on his radio.

'And for what it's worth, you have everything they're looking for anyway. They'll probably never check your exam grades and find out you faked half of them.'

Doug glanced across at his colleague and then back at Michael. He looked utterly caught out. It had been easy to pluck the guilty secret out of his head.

'I would put it out of your mind,' said Michael. 'It's not worth all the stress. Put it away now. And see your mum soon. She's not well.'

The radio went off again and the shocked officer snapped his attention to it. He moved away from Michael and turned his back. Even so, Michael could see the goosepimples that had risen across the man's neck and forearms. He'd had a seven star moment there and no mistake.

OK then, Sean—thank you! But is there any more on Lisa and Stacey? What can you give me?

Red river, said Sean, again. *Iron bracelets. East. You are closer. Purple blooms and concrete.* He sent an image into Michael's mind; a watery passage beneath high growing weeds.

'We're looking for a little inlet—somewhere

industrial!' he shouted, grabbing hold of Doug's shoulder. 'Overgrown with weeds and bushes.' He felt exhilaration flood through him. This was *real*! He was getting real spirit help. He could save them!

The launch engine suddenly cut down to a low idle and the vessel slowed abruptly, settling flat onto the river and turning in a wide arc. Michael repeated his instructions, assuming they needed to hear him more clearly, and waving energetically at the helmsman to turn back again and move on fast. But the man he'd mind-read clipped his radio back onto his belt and shook his head.

'We've just heard from Mr Volkov's people,' he said, one eyebrow raised. 'Seems his daughter is at home with him right now.'

'What?' gasped Michael, gripping the low rail of the launch hard.

'She's safe at home, Mr O'Flanagan,' went on Doug, eyeing him coldly now. 'So suppose you tell us what's really going on, eh?'

'I—I—he's lying!' Michael heard the words coming out as a squawk and even he knew it was hopeless. He sounded like an idiot. 'He must be saying that to keep her safe from harm . . . if the kidnappers have been in touch. Has anybody actually *seen* her with him? Send someone round to see her!'

'Mr O'Flanagan, are you aware who Mr Volkov *is*?' said Doug. 'He is a Russian diplomat. You don't get him for parking on a double yellow. You can't do him for speeding. You definitely don't get to show up at his gaff and demand to eyeball his daughter on the say-so of some celebrity mind-reading act. I'll tell you what we *can* do, though . . . '

'What?' mumbled Michael, feeling weak.

'We can arrest you for wasting police time!' grinned Doug. 'And maybe get the nick's duty psychiatrist in to have a word with you.'

'It'll go down a storm in *Heat* magazine,' observed his fellow officer.

'Wait! It's not just her! There's another girl missing too . . . another medium, like me! We have to keep going!' spluttered Michael, his heart going into a freefall of panic. His career about to hit the rocks was one thing, but . . . *red river, bracelets of iron,* dear God in heaven, he could not leave Lisa to that!

But the launch was already turning back west, the officers no longer even bothering to make eye contact with him. Again, Michael grabbed Doug by the shoulder. '*Please!*' he begged. 'You know I am a real psychic. *You* know! I am telling you the truth. Two girls are in terrible danger. How will you forgive yourself if they turn up dead in the river?'

'Sir,' said Doug, and his eyes were flat and out of reach, 'I do not want to have to cuff you, but if necessary, I will.'

'Read my mind.' Stacey's voice was a peculiar mixture of curiosity and fear. 'Go on. It'll pass the time.'

'I don't do party pieces,' muttered Lisa, but she sighed and decided she might as well. Most people's heads were easy to pop into if she chose to. (She rarely chose.) Some were harder, particularly those who were themselves psychic enough to realize that their thoughts were being rummaged through without their consent. Dax Jones, with his animal senses, could shut his mind off from her if he wanted. And many people, although they were not aware of it, possessed the power to close down the shutters to some degree. Most, though, were endlessly fascinated about themselves and agog to hear what a psychic might dig up. If they were willing it was as easy as strolling into an open house and helping herself to anything she liked.

Stacey's mind was certainly a stroll. She was pretty much what Lisa had already worked out—a fairly nice girl with a better brain than she knew. Her father adored her. Her mother loved her too, but was now with another husband and rather detached. Stacey would have benefited from a brother or sister to absorb some of her father's adoration—she was too spoilt to work at anything.

'You're bored out of your skull, you know,' said Lisa, a few seconds after taking the girl's cold damp hand.

'Bored? Are you kidding me?'

'Not here—not today,' went on Lisa. 'Just . . . generally. You're brighter than you realize and you should be doing something more than just shopping to Olympic standard. You should be . . . working with animals, probably. Or maybe working with kids and sport. You're good at sports . . . you did well at your school didn't you? Throwing stuff.'

'Oh yes!' said Stacey. 'I was top in discus and javelin in athletics. And I'm pretty amazing at frisbee. Tolstoy loves it when I throw frisbee for him on the beach . . . Well . . . he did.' She took a long breath and exhaled again before adding, 'Go on.'

'You're nuts about Michael O'Flanagan,' said

Lisa, feeling an odd little twist inside her as she spoke. 'But I didn't need to read your mind to know that. You're also nuts about three other good looking men in your life, but your dad doesn't approve of them. I don't think Prince William would be good enough for you as far as your dad's concerned.'

Stacey laughed and nodded in the darkness. 'Well, he's taken anyway,' she said.

Lisa went on. 'You had an ear infection when you were six and it was so bad you nearly died.' Stacey let out a gasp of astonishment. 'And you still can't hear quite so well in your right ear.'

'That's amazing!' marvelled the girl. Lisa was just about to add a few more insignificant but unknowable details when there was a scraping noise above them and a belt of fear shot through from Stacey's mind to hers.

'They're coming back,' whispered the girl, gripping her hand tighter.

Lisa shook her off and sat up on the floating wooden platform, her own heart beginning to race. *Now what, Sylv?*

Oh hell, sent back Sylv. *Wait! I'm getting help for you, my love. Hold on!*

My love? thought Lisa. Oh hell, indeed. Sylv only

ever used endearments like that when she felt *very* bad.

A man and a woman were coming along the walkway above them, carrying torches which sent dazzling beams in all directions as they walked. It was impossible to make out their faces. As they approached a woman's voice called out, 'OK, princess. Time to get going.'

'Edwina!' Stacey sounded appalled and angry. 'I *thought* it was you! Then I thought I must have dreamt it. I couldn't believe you would betray me. But here you are . . . '

'Oh, save it,' said the woman. 'Life's tough. People aren't always nice. Get over it.'

'Where are you taking me? Why are you doing this?'

'You know, you sound just like one of those kids in *Scooby Doo*,' said Edwina, with a cold laugh. 'Why—it couldn't be old lady Eddie? I would never have guessed! What? How? Why?' She set her torch down and knelt on the edge of the walkway and Lisa saw a heavy-jawed face, eyes glittering with malice and mouth set in a thin smile. 'And now you expect me to tell you my master plan. Well, honey, I'm not *that* dumb. All you need to know is that making a fuss will get you hurt. We said we'd give you back to Daddy if he did as he was told—but we didn't make any promises that you'd be given back all in one piece. We might send you home in stages, by second class post.'

Stacey took in a ragged breath as the man leaned over and grabbed her wrists, tugging them upwards and swiftly unlocking the metal cuffs around them.

'Wh-what about her?' Stacey said, nodding towards Lisa as the cuffs and chains dropped onto the pontoon with a clunk and a rattle. 'She's done nothing to upset you. You should let her go.'

Sergei grabbed her arms and hauled her up onto the walkway where a new set of cuffs was applied to her chafing wrists.

'She is of no interest to me,' said Edwina. 'She can stay here.'

'What—you're just going to leave her here?' Stacey sounded so horrified that Lisa felt guilty for judging her so harshly when they had first met. 'That's . . . inhuman.'

'Don't worry,' smiled Edwina. 'Sergei is going to give her a little something to help her sleep.'

Stacey began to yell something in Russian but

was borne away by Edwina, up some steps to a floor above, leaving only Sergei in the dank boatshed, peering at Lisa as she gripped the edge of the pontoon and tried to stay calm. This did not look good. Sylv had called her 'my love' and there had been a world of sorrow in those two words. Maybe this was how it ended for her.

'You're going to kill me, aren't you?' she said and Sergei shrugged and dropped his eyes to the water.

'I do not wish to,' he said. 'Some things I must do.'

Sylv, sent Lisa. *Now would be a good time to help!*

Read him! yelled back Sylv, sounding stressed and distracted, as if she was in hand-to-hand combat with someone. *Stall him! I'm sending someone! Start with Marsha!*

Lisa closed her eyes briefly, as Sergei lowered his legs from the walkway and prepared to jump down to her. She got what she needed fast. 'Marsha says hello,' she said, and the man froze.

'What?' he said.

'Marsha. She says hello. And she hopes you will think of another way.' Lisa stared up at the man. In the torchlight she could not see the blood drain from his face, but she felt it. She pressed on, her heart crashing in her chest, knowing that her mediumship was the last chance she had to hang on to her life. 'She died when she was twelve—of meningitis. You were her favourite brother. She says you visit her grave every year on her birthday. She likes the yellow flowers you bring. Yellow is her favourite colour.'

'Stop,' said the man, hoarsely. 'What the hell *are* you?'

'What the hell are *you?*' Lisa bit back. She could sense that he was not the monster that Edwina was, and this made her angry. 'Marsha is wondering that too!'

'You . . . this is a trick!' he spat. 'You have information on me! Who sent you?'

'I'm a psychic medium,' said Lisa. 'And yes—I *do* have information on you. Marsha says you are a good man and you don't want to kill me. She says you're trying to do something for your country. She says you're wrong. You're doing it all the wrong way. She sa—'

She was cut off abruptly as Sergei struck her across the face. 'Shut up!' he yelled. 'Shut up! Shut up!'

The pontoon rocked wildly as he leapt down onto it and grabbed her head, one hand over her mouth and the other at her throat. Lisa tried to claw at him but her wrists were snagged down again by the chains. She screamed but the sound barely made it out through his thick hot fingers. *My love,* Sylv had said. *My love.* She knew it was all over. He was going to break her neck.

12

There were press photographers at the bank when the police launch pulled in. Michael could barely believe it. *One* lousy freelancer at his book signing. Six or seven paparazzi *now*—jostling for space at the water's edge, their motorbikes parked up at the roadside above. Clearly somebody had tipped off the media. The launch berthed on the north side of the river and the press pack surged towards him.

'Michael! Michael! Mystic Mike! Hey—Mike! What's going on? Have you helped to solve a kidnapping? Are you involved? Mike! Who's the missing teenage girl? Is she your girlfriend? Michael—do you have an under-age girlfriend?' The flashbulbs were popping like a firework display, even though it was a bright late afternoon.

'Michael,' cried one joker. 'Did you see this coming?'

The officers began to guide him off the launch, but he didn't step out. Instead he turned away from the bank and looked from one to the other. 'You've nothing to charge me with apart from wasting police time,' he stated and did a quick read of their responses. He knew he was right.

'Doug,' he said, touching the officer's arm. 'I think you really don't want to do this, do you? It's a lot of paperwork for nothing. Let me go on now, and let's leave it at that, shall we?'

Doug glanced at his colleague and then back at Michael, considering.

'I mean . . . we all make mistakes, don't we?' Michael stared hard at him and increased the pressure on his arm. 'It's not like any of us are perfect, is it?' He saw the flash of fear in the man's eyes. Doug knew O'Flanagan could easily prompt an investigation into his little white lie about his exam grades. Was it worth it? The fun of having a celebrity in the cells wasn't really enough to justify endangering his career, surely?

'Mr O'Flanagan,' Doug said, in his officer's tone, 'we will be allowing you to leave with a caution

143

today—but the next time you waste police time we won't be so forgiving about it, do you understand me?'

Michael fixed the man with a look that said, yes, he understood—they both understood. He released his grip. The transaction was complete.

'Go on then, sir.'

Michael clambered onto the shore and waved at the photographers. 'Nothing to see here, boys,' he grinned. 'Move along now.' He knew they wouldn't, of course. The paps had a sixth sense almost as good as his when it came to bit of scandal. Their questions rose up again but this time Michael stood and absorbed it all. He locked on to each of the faces and voices in turn, searching for his man. Finally, he found him.

'Jason,' he said, doing his direct hazel-brown stare special at the young snapper on his right.

The man lowered his Nikon and blinked, surprised and amused. 'Yeah?' Immediately the others turned their lenses, to catch the conversation between the two men.

'You're with the *Sun*, yes?'

Jason glanced at his fellow photographers, wondering if one of them had set him up.

'Yeah,' he said, cautiously.

'I want to do an exclusive,' said Michael. 'With you.'

A storm of protest rose. 'Hey! What gives? You've not given us a chance to bid!' Some were on mobile phones, in touch with their newsdesks, already negotiating sums for this story—a story they had no details on apart from a police chase up the Thames and a missing teenage girl and a telly celebrity. It was certainly enough.

'You,' said Michael, pointing at the *Sun* photographer, ignoring offers of £50,000, £75,000, £100,000. 'Exclusive—but only if we go now. Right now—to the location of my choice.'

'I have to call in,' said Jason, digging for his mobile. 'They'll want to send a reporter.'

'You come with me now—we'll call your newsdesk when we get there. Tell them,' he waved at the rest of the posse, 'tell them it's agreed.'

Jason took a deep breath and then turned and shrugged at the others. 'We're agreed. It's exclusive to the *Sun*. Forget it, boys.' There was another howl of protest but Michael didn't wait to listen.

'Now!' he said, climbing fast up the bank and hoping there was a spare helmet on the back of the young man's Triumph. There was. As he clambered on behind, pulling the helmet over his wild hair, he hoped Sean had steered him right. Jason was a former motocross champion. If anyone could get him away from here and back along the eastern stretch of the Thames, while outrunning the rest of the press, this man could.

The engine roared into life. 'Where are we going?' Jason shouted back to him. Michael sensed his surge of adrenalin and excitement and knew he'd picked the right man.

'East,' he said. 'I'll tell you as we go.'

She thought of Dax. She thought of Mia and Gideon and her father. She could not form a goodbye in her head for them as Sergei's fingers folded around her jaw and prepared to snap it sideways. There was no time left.

Lisa! Make him look! Make him LOOK! Sylv suddenly bawled in her ear.

Lisa stopped senselessly fighting her chains and instead raised a shaky finger, pointing at the figure which was walking through the water towards them. It worked. Sergei still held her, but as he glanced in the direction his victim was pointing, the intent abruptly left his hands.

A man stood in the water. He was wearing a business suit. Half of his face blown away and blood draining from the remaining mess like water from a broken dam. '*You* did this,' he said, in spite of having only half a mouth, his one eye fixed upon Sergei. '*You* did this.'

She felt the shudder go through the man's chest and into her shoulders. She heard him give a gurgling cry of horror as the hideous ruin of the man he had once killed (three years ago, in a Ukrainian wood, her talent swiftly informed her) drifted closer to him, making no ripples in the water, although its lower half was deep in it. She felt his hands leave her face and rise to his own as he tried to hide from the advancing ghoul.

His words, when they began to spill in horrified gasps from his mouth, were in Russian, but her psychic mind provided an instant translation.

'No! No! Alexei—no! I had to. I had no choice. Forgive me! No! Don't—oh, don't!'

Lisa cried out as the spirit of Alexei passed right through her, leaving a chilled wake of nausea in her belly before enveloping Sergei, who was scrabbling wildly in the air and trying to back away from it. The pontoon tilted violently and he fell backwards into the water, still scrabbling and shrieking, and even at that speed Lisa could see the spirit kneeling on his chest, clinging fast to him and pressing its half a face into his whole one. As Lisa tumbled off the pontoon into the cold slick blackness, she saw Sergei submerge with a sharp jerk. His drowned screams rose to the surface in a torrent of bubbles. One hand flailed out and grabbed the chain which had held Stacey. Another hand—a spirit hand—guided it. The chain spun and spiralled like an agonized sea serpent and Sergei's face bloomed up through the water, eyes wide and horrified, as the metal links wrapped around his neck. And tightened.

Lisa tried to get away but she could only turn her head. She felt the water churning around her as the man's limbs kicked and flailed. His fight seemed to go on for ever, and then one free hand grabbed at her ankle, tugging her towards him. She kicked it away, screaming. The dying fingers did not find her again as she clung to the chains and the edge of the pontoon, screwing her eyes shut and pressing her lips tightly together. The struggling grew slower and the flailing weakened. Eventually the water stopped churning and simply rose and fell to the left and the right, slopping and sighing, each time with less energy, until it was all but still again. Lisa gripped the edge of the unstable platform, allowing her legs to drift up to a floating position and letting her cheek rest on the rough wood. She kept her eyes shut for fifteen minutes. She knew how it would look anyway—the spirit version was bobbing mercilessly behind her closed eyelids. The man once known as Sergei lay an inch or two beneath the water, his eyes bulging with something more like apology than fear, his mouth slack and his thin hair waving like fronds of underwater weed.

When she finally opened her eyes, the scene was exactly this.

Don't be sick, she told herself. *I know you want to hurl it all out of you but that won't help. You'll be dehydrated. You don't need that, on top of everything else.*

Well done, love, said Sylv, close inside her head, her voice filled with emotion.

Where did you find that half headed freak? wondered Lisa.

It wasn't easy, muttered Sylv. *It took all the energy I had to haul him across the threshold and make him put on a show.*

A show? He murdered a human being from beyond the grave! I didn't think that was even possible! Not that I'm not . . . appreciative, she added.

It's rare. Not impossible.

So. Lisa tried to sound bright and business-like as she trod water. *What next?*

Michael was coming to help, said Sylv. *But now he's not coming.* Her voice was very weak in Lisa's head and she knew that Sylv had been quite factual about how much energy she had just used.

Wait! Sylv! You're fading! Please don't go. What should I do? Lisa heard the panic in her internal voice and it sent shudders through her. She was chained to a bit of wood, stuck alone in a deserted boatshed with just a corpse for company and '*he's not coming*'?

No energy. Will come back. Won't leave you . . . promi—

Sylv was gone. Not for ever. Lisa knew she would come back—but not *when*. Sylv had never had to burn up that much energy for her before. Lisa did not know whether it would take her hours to recharge—or days. Or weeks.

13

The motorbike moved in and out of the crawling London traffic with speed and precision. Michael's heart had been hammering before they'd even pulled away from the riverside and it wasn't slowing down at all. A street or two behind, the rest of the motorbike-riding paparazzi were attempting to keep up, but with each passing minute his champion rider put more space between them.

'Where now?' the man shouted as they reached a busy crossroads.

'Right!' yelled back Michael, and the bike pulled sharply away. He hoped the straps on the backpack the man was wearing were as strong as they looked—he was clinging on to it for dear life. It was full of very expensive Nikon equipment—it had to be strong, he told himself, shifting his weight instinctively as the Triumph cornered tightly and powered on down a bus lane.

'How much further?' Jason called back.

Michael had no idea. He could sense that Stacey was still in London; still within a half hour radius—but exactly where? No clue. Sean was guiding him road by road and they'd been travelling for nearly fifteen minutes now, but the route was odd and wandering. Did his spirit guide really have any idea where Stacey and Lisa were? Assuming they were together, of course. They might not be.

'How far?' Jason called again.

'Keep going!' he shouted back. 'Won't be long now.'

He was right. As they turned down a narrow side road, Sean started yelling in his head: *LEFT! LEFT! LEFT! LEFT!*

But this is Tower Hamlets! We're nowhere near the Thames!

I'm telling you, said Sean. *LEFT! And UP.*

Michael shouted to the photographer to pull over as he stared up to the left. Above him loomed a six-storey block of flats. The grey boxy style spoke of the 1960s, although some 1980s updating had gone on, with narrow metal ridges running up the side of the building, like an enormous red radiator, in an attempt to lend it some style. *They're in there? You've got to be kidding me!*

Just arrived, sent back Sean. *They had to move Stacey from the watery place.*

No Lisa? Michael felt his chest tighten with anxiety.

No Lisa.

OK—one thing at a time then—where is Stacey?

In the building.

'SEAN! There are six floors!' Michael yelled aloud, as Jason stopped the engine.

'You what?' said Jason.

I'm working on it, insisted Sean.

Michael got off the bike, his legs shaking from the stress of staying on the pillion and the fear—yes, certainly fear. He was no hero. Even if they could find the right flat, he wasn't equipped to run in there and save a kidnapped girl with nothing but a pap and a spirit guide for company. But what else was he to do?

'When you're ready, Sean,' he sighed, wishing he hadn't burnt his boats with the police. *Back-up.* What a lovely, hopeless pair of words. But he had no back-up. And no plan.

'Who were you talking to?' asked Jason as he took the spare helmet to lock it to the bike.

'My spirit guide,' sighed Michael. 'Oh—can I keep that with me?' He took back the shiny black helmet, instinct telling him it might be needed.

'Oh right—your spirit guide,' grinned the photographer, letting his spare helmet go. 'Of course. Now can I call newsdesk?'

'Once we're inside,' said Michael.

'OK—let's go inside,' said the photographer with a tight smile. 'Then I make the call. This better be front page lead.'

'Oh, I think you're safe on that count, whatever happens,' gulped Michael. *Top floor,* sent Sean. *Take the stairs—they're watching the lift. They're armed. Very armed.*

'Top floor,' he relayed to Jason. 'Do exactly as I say and we might get out of this alive.'

'You telly types are such drama queens,' chuckled Jason, shaking his head.

After an hour, when her heartbeat had returned to normal and the cold of the water began to make her shiver instead of just the horror, Lisa noticed something unpleasant. Something *else* unpleasant. As if being trapped at close quarters with a semi-submerged dead body and some increasingly daring rats wasn't bad enough, she began to find it difficult to rest her head on the edge of the wooden pontoon. The platform was higher than before.

She had tried several times to climb back onto it, but she was exhausted and weighed down by soaked clothes and her feet could not reach the bed of this river inlet to give her any push-away. And her arms were heavy with the chains. She realized that her wrist cuffs were linked to a chain which was also linked to the one Stacey had been attached to—which was now snagged around the throat of the dead man once known as Sergei. And as Sergei's body took on more water, it was slowly sinking and dragging the chain down with it. This was only part of the problem. The other part was that the tide was coming in.

Glancing up in the light of the torch which her would-be killer had left up on the walkway, Lisa could see dripping green and black algae and weed clumping on the walls around her. It showed a clear, recent high tide mark about a metre above her current head-height. On the pontoon she would have simply risen up with it, but now she was anchored by the dead, sponge-like weight of the late Sergei and rising was no longer an option.

I'm going to drown, she realized. If that Edwina woman didn't come back and kill her first, that was. After all, she had to have noticed that Sergei had not followed on. She had to wonder why. She didn't seem like the type to leave any loose ends. So . . . death by broken neck, or drowning? Hmmm. What to choose?

Oh hell, she whimpered. *Sylv? Are you there?* Nothing. Sylv was well and truly spent. She wondered why the usual crowd of spirits wasn't tumbling in to her head without Sylv to hold them off, and then realized that maybe the holding off was all that Sylv *could* do for her right now.

OK, girl. Think. You need help. Send for it. Try for Michael—you never know—he might be nearby. He might pick up a telepathic signal! He might! She sent one—loud and clear and ringing with fear. Nothing came back. No psychic response—not even a tingle. *OK. How about Dax?* 'He's three hundred miles away!' she told the rats, making them scurry away to the darker edges of the water. 'I've never tried to contact his mind across that kind of distance without something to link us! I always made a connection first . . . with a phone line or through one of the other Colas. I don't have a hope!'

Try anyway, advised another part of her head, which sounded like Mia. If he's shifted to a fox or falcon right now, you might stand a chance. She tried. *DAX! DAX! DAX! HELP! I'M IN DANGER! I'M GOING TO DROWN! PLEASE HELP ME!* She quietened her mind, waiting desperately for some kind of psychic ping back—anything at all. For several seconds she held her breath, hope ebbing away. Then there was a sudden smell of hot sausage in her nose. Hot and drenched with gravy, alongside buttery mashed potato; one of Mrs M's specialities at Fenton Lodge where she lived with Dax and the other Children of Limitless Ability. *Limitless.* Oh, she really hoped so. *DAX? DAX? Are you sending me that?* Nothing followed. Maybe it was just her own tired psyche finding a way to comfort her in her final hour. The water was at her chin now. She shut her mouth, thinking of that water-borne disease that rats carried. What was it? Weil's Disease, she thought. Oh good-oh!

It was the sausages that made the difference. Without them he would never have picked up the call because he would have been human when it came. Sausages were Dax's favourite. Three hundred miles away in the remotest part of the Lake District, Dax Jones walked into the dining room of Fenton Lodge and grinned.

'Ooooh! Cumbrian sausage! My favourite. Hang on a minute, Gid. I've got to have the full effect.'

Even though it was against the rules in the dining room, he shifted quickly to DaxFox and at once a wave of intense sausage scent engulfed him, fox smell being off the scale compared to the human sense. It was enough to make his whiskers quiver.

Gideon wrinkled his freckled nose and raised an eyebrow at his best friend. 'You know—that's very selfish. You're getting a full-on sausage sniffing bonanza which I can never hope to experience. You don't have to look quite so pleased with yourself.'

Dax was a moment away from shifting back so he could pick up a plate when a dark gust of horror blew him sideways. He literally slid off his paws and thudded against the wall. Gideon saw the fox's eyes go suddenly opaque and distant and he dropped to his knees, assailed by fear.

'Dax! What is it?'

The fox stared into the air, seeing nothing of the

dining room as it filled up with hungry Colas. Dax's breath was coming fast and shallow. He could smell brackish water, rats and water voles, old concrete and brick, wet, mouldering wood and . . . death. Human death. Recent. And . . . oh no . . . Lisa. He could smell Lisa and he could smell her fear.

He was back in boy form in an instant, and running out of the dining room at speed, beckoning to Gideon to follow him.

'What? What?' panted Gideon, racing up the stairs behind Dax. 'What's going on?'

Dax didn't speak until he reached their bedroom. 'It's Lisa,' he said, a thick sound to the words as his throat was constricting with fear. 'She's in very bad trouble. She's calling me.'

'What? Where is she? She's meant to be on a girly shopping trip with Mia!' gasped Gideon.

'Well, she's not,' said Dax, flinging up the sash window and then swiping some money and a bar of Gideon's chocolate from the deep window sill and shoving it into his jeans pockets.

'Where are you going?' Gideon was looking pale and scared now.

'South. To London,' said Dax, turning to him. 'I have to get closer to her so I can hear her words.

I'm only getting feelings and smells right now.'

'Shouldn't we tell the principal?' said Gideon. 'Mrs Sartre will know what to do.'

'No,' said Dax. 'There is no time. They'll ground me if they can—and then it'll be too late for Lisa.'

'But you've got trackers in your clothes,' said Gideon. 'They'll track you and follow.'

'I know—they might. And maybe that's a good thing—Lisa might need them,' said Dax. 'But they can't stop me if I go now. Bye, mate. Wish me luck.'

'Good luck,' gulped Gideon.

Dax paused before shifting. 'Gid,' he said, narrowing his eyes as an idea hit him. 'Can you . . . push me?'

'You what?'

'Push me—push me south! I can fly faster than any other bird. Faster than normal peregrines . . . but I need to get to London *really* fast. Can you push me with your mind?'

Gideon stared at him. He had moved people before, but the telekinesis had only ever worked properly before now on people who were not fully conscious; not in charge of their own limbs. 'I can try,' he said. 'I *will* try—but I don't know if it'll work. You'll have to somehow *let* it work . . . accept it.'

'It's worth a try,' said Dax. He gulped. 'Because I really don't think there's much time. You might have to keep it up for a while . . . can you do that? Half an hour, maybe? And then tell Mrs Sartre— call in Control—raise hell!'

Gideon nodded and sat on his bed while his best friend shifted to a falcon. The falcon exchanged a yellow-rimmed stare with the boy for a few seconds and then flew off the sill into the twilight. Gideon visualized his power—a silver pulsing stream of great intensity—and pictured it following behind the falcon, pushing the bird fast ahead, like a following wind. He felt the connection and held it firm in his mind.

High above the fells a peregrine falcon cheated the laws of physics as it shot through the early evening thermals at something approaching four hundred miles per hour.

The water was lapping at her lower lip now, and she had to keep her mouth tightly shut. She had tried three times now to dive down and get to the pocket of the dead man's jacket. She had seen him put the key to Stacey's cuffs in there. If she could just get it and somehow use it in her own cuffs . . . but she could not reach before the chains at her wrists held her back. She tried stretching through the dark water with her feet, having kicked off the running shoes, which bobbed to the surface of the water, but could only reach as far as the drowned head. The hair tickled her toes repulsively and then the head bobbed away. Oh, what she would *give* to have Gideon's telekinetic power right now. She could float the key out and make it do her bidding. But she was sunk—very nearly literally. The water was rising ever higher and she now had to tilt her head back to keep it clear of her nostrils.

Oh Dax! she whimpered in her head. *I wish you could hear me. I wish you could help. I wish anyone could help.* She felt a surge of anger against Michael for getting her into this and then just opting out. She could not imagine what had become of him, but she kept picturing him shrugging and going on his way after a cursory search along the river bank. Part of her knew it was unfair—she had read decency and courage in him, behind his puffed-up ego. But where was he now? Probably going after Stacey if he was still going after anyone at all. She was his client, after all—and her dad was rich and powerful.

Nobody's coming, girl, she told herself, sadly. *No help for you. It doesn't work like that, does it? Colas get to do all the sacrifice and mustn't ever expect anything in return.* She shouted out in frustration and it came out as a sob, cut off suddenly by a peak of choppy dark water which slopped across her mouth. She tilted her head up further, snatching a lungful of air while she still could.

'Why me?' she yelled, as fury spiralled up through her chest. 'Why do I have to be left here? Left here to die in the dark? WHY? What have I done? Why should I be abandoned here? Left! Why? Where is MY rescue?'

A bluish light filled the room, sending bright sapphires dancing across the water. Lisa twisted in her chains, staring in the direction of the phantom glow. She felt her eyes stretch wide in absolute amazement.

'You?'

Drifting towards her was the spirit girl in the soaked nightgown—the ghost she had been ignoring at the hotel for the past three days.

'Left,' said the girl. 'Abandoned.' She raised her thin arms and the frayed bangles of rope still swung there.

Lisa let out a wild laugh. 'Have you come to gloat?' she yelled. 'Or just to guide me over to the other side? Serves me right, does it?'

'Tell me who to reach,' said the girl and Lisa nearly choked as her mouth went into automatic gape mode. 'Channel through me—who shall I go to?'

'Michael O'Flanagan!' Lisa spluttered. 'He's a medium like me—but he doesn't do so well on telepathy. He should see or hear you, though. Tell him—show him where I am!'

The spirit nodded and smiled sadly, more dark river water streaming through her dead mouth.

'And Dax!' yelled Lisa, tilting her head back up again as the water threatened to engulf her. 'Try Dax Jones! Please! Ask Sylv to guide you!'

The girl nodded again and began to fade away. 'Thank you!' called Lisa, for the first time ever to a spirit person aside from Sylv. 'And hurry!'

14

Edwina snapped her mobile phone shut and glared at it. 'Still going to voicemail,' she told the two men who leaned against the mildew-patterned wall of the living room. 'Where the hell is he?'

'Sergei was to go to the theatre viewpoint, yes?' asked Anton, moving to grasp the back of an ancient stained sofa.

'Yes,' said Edwina. 'To set up the live link in the building opposite, and relay the death of the Prime Minister for your boss's delight. We have no reason to assume he is not in place—except that we can't raise him and he is twelve minutes late in checking in. I am not happy. Not happy at all. Anton—you'll have to go there. You remember where to go? Find out for sure. We need to show your people the assassination as soon as it happens. I catch my flight an hour later. I cannot be late.'

'It is good that I go,' said Anton, his eyes growing intense as the bearded older man beside him nodded. 'If Volkov fails I can shoot.'

'Volkov won't fail,' said Edwina, giving the young man a contemptuous glare. 'He is fully equipped and in no doubt what will happen to his daughter if he doesn't do as he's told. And if you think you can shoot the British Prime Minister on a whim you're a bigger idiot than you look. This has taken nearly a year to put into place—it's perfect and it's self cleaning. It will work. The PM will die in front of the world's press, Volkov will be blamed, your sad little Radachnyan army will have a big party and I will get my pay off.'

'And the girl—what will she get?' grinned Peter, the bearded man, nodding towards the kitchen where Stacey lay inside a roll of carpet, her mouth taped up, unable to move.

'A quick drop over the balcony, if she's lucky,' grunted Edwina. 'No . . . I've done quite enough babysitting of that one. I can finish her in that carpet and leave the body here. It will be days before anyone comes to investigate the smell. It'll be one nasty spring roll.'

She was in a bad mood. The back-up plan of the safe house had always been an option, but she was rattled that they had needed it. She had kept Stacey awake, but bound and gagged in the back of the Transit van. At the block of flats she had gone on ahead, letting herself into the flat with a clipboard in her hand and the jacket and professional smile of a property developer. Ten minutes later Peter and Anton had carried the girl upstairs, knocked out again and wrapped in a carpet. Just two guys delivering to a top floor flat undergoing refurbishment. Nobody bothered about them. It was chancier than she liked, but it helped to know that Volkov had gone along with their demands about not involving the police. His paid former MI5 minders were incapable of speaking, even if they were still alive. Nobody should be looking for Stacey yet.

But where had that blonde girl come from? Maybe she'd given that information away to Sergei in the last moments as she begged for her life. Edwina hoped Sergei had had the sense to weigh down the body and sink it. If anyone did manage to follow their trail as far as the boatshed it would make her life much easier if a dead lump of teenage evidence *wasn't* floating there for all to see. She would have interrogated the girl herself had there been time—but it wasn't going to matter soon. The clock was ticking—the plan was moving on. Soon she would be flying to a new life in South America, weighed down by £2 million in used bank notes.

Anton holstered a Makarov semi automatic inside his casual leather jacket and headed for the door. 'I will call you as soon as I get there,' he promised.

He stepped outside the flat, looking left and right in the deepening shade of the early evening, and sniffed in a sharp, satisfied breath. Whatever that English shrew thought, he was quite willing to chance a shot at the Prime Minister if it became necessary. The Makarov would do at a push but at the theatre viewpoint there was a Draganov SVD sniper begging for some use. His belly tightened at the thought of it and a humourless smile flashed across his face. Using the SVD would not be as good as Volkov himself doing the deed, but still very damning for the Russian government's fragile relationship with Britain and the west. And if it *did* all go to plan he would take great pleasure in being at Sergei's side and witnessing the live show of the Russian ambassador finishing off the British leader. He wanted to be in at the kill, not guarding some stupid girl whom they were going to despatch anyway as soon as they had what they wanted. This was going his way.

As he strode along the balcony walkway he glanced through the heavy net curtains of a window into the well-lit sitting room where a couple sat gawping at a television, eating convenience dinners off their laps. They did not return his glance but went on chewing and staring like cattle. He sneered at the London people, living here in this block of flats, completely clueless and making an art form out of dumb ignorance. Nobody in his home town would be so dull and sheep-like while wolves such as he prowled their lanes. He knew these people would all deny seeing him if the police ever showed up to ask. 'Not my problem, mate,' was the catchphrase around here. They were spineless and contemptible, with their soap opera addictions and their gutter press and their shallow TV celebrities—

As Anton swung quickly around the iron banister and down into the dark chimney of the concrete stairwell his thoughts ended abruptly in a searing white flash of light and a sudden impact which broke his nose. He'd been blinded by a member of the gutter press and knocked unconscious by a shallow TV celebrity.

Dax Jones could see the glow of London beneath him—a vast pool of light twinkling up from the basin of land that fell to the Thames. He felt his heartbeat rise to a thrum as excitement and fear flooded his falcon frame. What if he couldn't find Lisa, now? What if she did not send him another signal? What if he was already too late?

You're not too late. Not yet, said a voice in his head. Not a voice he recognized and yet in the same second he knew—much to his surprise—that it was a girl spirit. *The river. Go east along the river.* The spirit (around Lisa's age, he suddenly knew) sent an image to him next—a bird's eye view of some derelict land by a river—an old concrete hard with a boathouse and a thin snaking inlet of water.

He stooped, plummeting towards the meandering loops of the River Thames, before turning east and levelling out to speed along at thirty metres above the water. Gideon's telekinetic push had begun to wear off after around twenty minutes, but it had given an incredible boost to his phenomenal natural speed. He should have stopped before now to eat the chocolate he'd pocketed—by rights he should be completely out of fuel. But now he shot along with renewed energy and realized that the spirit who had communicated with him had given him a boost too. Clearly the inhabitants of the spirit world did not want Lisa to join them today.

Lisa! Lisa! Lisa! He sent his mental call down towards the river as his astonishingly sharp eyes picked out every detail in the fading light, scanning for a replica of the image the spirit had sent him. *Lisa! Where are you?*

What he got back was a sense of grey, exhausted dread and worse . . . of giving up.

'What the *hell*? Are you nuts?' squawked Jason, staring over the top of his camera at the man who lay crumpled on the concrete steps at the psychic guy's feet.

Michael gripped the bike helmet and stared from its shiny curve to the bleeding face of his victim. *That's one—one of three,* Sean told him. *Don't feel guilty. He's a vicious murderer.*

'No—I'm not nuts,' muttered Michael, feeling queasy with shock. He'd been in many fights in his youth and was no stranger to a bit of violence, but he'd never knocked anyone out cold. 'This is one of three very bad people who've kidnapped a teenage girl.'

The photographer gawped at him, fear and doubt chasing across his face.

'Help me,' said Michael. 'If you want to save the girl.' He grabbed the unconscious man and dragged him, thudding the unconscious body from step to step, down to the next landing. There was a utility room there, behind a painted wooden door with an aged padlock on a rusty hasp. Michael kicked the padlock and hasp off in one go and pulled the door open. 'Help me!' he said again, but Jason was pulling out his mobile phone and jabbing at it, keeping a wary eye on Michael.

'Fine,' said Michael, grunting as he hefted the slumped-over body into the grimy utility room and shoved it against the wall.

He didn't need to check the man's pulse to know he was still alive, but his psychic sense told him that waking up was still some way off for this . . . Anton . . . that was his name. Arrogant, vicious . . . had killed four people and tortured many more. If it weren't for the legal complications, Michael would be quite glad if he *didn't* wake up. He checked inside the man's jacket and, with a cold thrill of horror, found a heavy metal gun; black with a nut-brown handle. He took it out carefully and put it in his jacket pocket where it weighed down the fine material considerably. He took it out again. He had no intention of firing it. He wanted it out of commission. He noticed a fire bucket filled with sand and old cigarette butts and swiftly buried the weapon in it, covering it completely. It would be wrecked by the sand even if it was found, he guessed.

Back on the landing the photographer was talking on the phone, looking around him edgily. 'Good,' said Michael. 'Call the police. Call your paparazzi mates. Call the world—get them here. Flat 57.'

Jason finished relaying the address and ended the call. 'What the hell is going on here?' he asked, his voice shaking and low.

'I told you. A girl has been kidnapped and if we don't do something, she's going to end up dead. Now . . . you've got a great photo of Mystic Mike assaulting a murderer. Is that enough for you? Will it fetch you much? Because, if you help me I think you can look at quadrupling your fee, so you can. Help me. Get into the story with me. I need you.'

'I—I've called the newsdesk. They're sending reporters,' Jason gulped.

Michael grinned, in spite of the dire situation they were in. Typical press. Newsdesk first. 'Well, I'm sure a crack team of Dictaphone wielding hacks can easily outsmart any cell of gun-toting mobsters. But, on the off-chance they *can't*—could you call the police now? And make them believe you, because they would not believe me. And even if they still don't buy it, they've got to come to arrest me, now, haven't they? Look what I just did!'

The man stared at him for a few seconds, his camera clutched against his chest like a shield and then he glanced up the stairs. 'Up there?' he said. 'A kidnapped girl is being held up there?'

Michael nodded. Jason pulled out his phone again and dialled 999, but even before he got through there were sirens and blue lights approaching. Michael ran to the edge of the stairwell and peered through a glassless window to see two squad cars sweeping into the car park below, accompanied by a convoy of motorbikes and a TV satellite van—the press.

Damn! he sent to Sean. *No chance of a subtle*

approach then. What if they just kill her and run? He ran up the stairwell past Jason, panic washing through every layer of his skin. At the top a corridor, open to the air on one side above a chest height brick wall, ran the length of seven or eight flats. Number 57 was the door at the very end. It was closed and the window beside it was dark. A chopping sound was getting louder in the air around him.

Flash! The door was lit up in a white flare. Michael turned round to see Jason taking photos of it.

'Are you mad?' he hissed. 'They're in there.'

'Not for long,' muttered Jason, just as the huge black helicopter loomed overhead. He took shots of that too as it went overhead, until Michael grabbed his arm and yanked him down into a low crouching position.

'They must be dropping rescuers on to the roof,' muttered Michael. 'The cavalry's here at last—but how come? Have you guys ever got the police *this* excited before?'

Jason shrugged. 'Don't ask me, mate. The biggest panic I ever shot was Britney Spears at Leicester Square. How do you know they're coming up here, even? Might be something else going on down there . . . '

He crept closer to the flat and attempted to look through the window via his Nikon. Three seconds later there was an explosion of glass and a thud and the photographer lay on his back, gasping, a ragged red hole in his shoulder.

'I . . . I've been shot,' he whispered, staring down at the wound in disbelief.

Michael crawled to him, his heart racing. 'Don't worry,' he hissed. 'They're coming. They'll get paramedics. Just stay down and keep quiet.' He glanced up at the shattered window above, expecting the muzzle of a gun to tilt over it and aim at him at any second. There was a louder thud above him and through the thick safety glass of a skylight in the balcony roof he saw black shapes, running low and silently. They had to be special operatives from that chopper, put down on the roof and coming to rescue Stacey, didn't they? Or were they more enemies? What the hell was he to do *now*?

Get his bike key! yelled Sean. *Now! Before it's too late!*

'What?' gasped Michael. Jason's eyes rolled up into his skull.

You have to go now, Sean said. *You can't do any more. Those men are the entry team. They'll arrest you too before you get a chance to say or do anything. Get his bike key.*

You need to get away before it's too late for Lisa. He'll be OK. He's not coming to us today.

Lisa! Michael felt a fresh belt of fear. He checked Jason for life signs as he rummaged in his pockets for the bike key. There was a lot of blood but it was high on his shoulder, nowhere near any vital organs. With help so close he should be fine . . . but Stacey?

What about Stacey? he called to Sean. *Is SHE coming to the spirit world today?*

No! But Lisa will if you don't move NOW. GO!

There was another muffled shot inside the flat as Michael grabbed the keys and ran for the stairwell, turning into it two seconds ahead of the zipwire men arriving on the wall of the balcony corridor behind him. *Are you SURE, Sean? There was another shot!* He scooped up the helmet from the blood spattered steps as he ran down, throwing it over his head and hoping it would be disguise enough from the paps and the police. *She's alive,* sent back Sean. *Go!* At the first floor he heard the sound of men approaching and jumped out of the glassless opening to one side of the stairwell, landing on plastic topped bins below. The crack of his feet hitting them was thankfully muffled by the noise of the chopper hovering above.

How he reached the bike without capture was a mystery to him later—maybe the helmet with its red *THE SUN* sticker, as well as the pap's bike, just helped him to melt into the press pack and then sidle away. Most of the press had arrived ahead of the police and were getting in the way of their attempts to create a cordon and handle panicked members of the public. A sleek operation it was not.

Let us in, said Sean, as soon as the Triumph engine was throttling up. *See what we see.* And for the first time in their partnership, Michael's spirit guide gave him a totally clear image of the route he must take. There had been hints and clues and instincts aplenty exchanged between them for seven years, but never with such clarity. *I'm three star now,* Michael thought, as the bike tore south, back towards the river. *And Sean has a friend!* For a grey-washed girl was holding hands with Sean somewhere in the spirit world, guiding them both. Not Lisa. Lisa was not in the spirit world. Not yet . . .

15

Desperation had won her a few more minutes. In fury she had pulled so hard on the chains that the wooden pontoon she and Stacey had shared flipped over in the water. It missed braining her by a hair's breadth, but something in its movement loosened a link or two of the chains and she was able to rise up just a little, so that her chin cleared the water again. It wouldn't make much difference in the end, though, she realized. The tide was still rising; she could tell from the pressure of water pushing in around her. Within five minutes it was back up to her mouth.

Around this time she felt the tickly sensation across her scalp which told her she was being dowsed. Almost certainly by Paulina Sartre, back at Fenton Lodge . . . maybe helped by some of the other Colas who had lesser powers. The principal was a powerful seer and dowser—although not off-the-scale like she herself was. A bitter smile wobbled across her tightly shut mouth. Too little, too late. Even the Cola Project's best crack team of rescuers couldn't make it here soon enough now.

Sylv . . . she called, the sound weak even inside her head. *Any hope? Or are we going to meet face to face today?*

Sylv at last responded—but was very faint. *Sending!* she called back. *Trying!*

Poor Sylv, doing her best to the last, Lisa acknowledged, sadly. Possibly connecting to the girl spirit who had turned up to offer help, much to her surprise. Who'd have thought it? Poor dead thing, being nice even after she'd been accused of having BO. Lisa was not afraid of being dead— she knew that there was plenty going on after that. But she feared the actual process of dying, here, like this. It would not be quick. And she bitterly resented it too. She wasn't even 16. The unfairness of it all was too much. And she would miss Mia. And Dax. Even Gideon and certainly Dad. Oh, and it would destroy poor Dad. Imagining his sorrow made her eyes well up and her mouth pucker. She heard herself whimper. The sound was smothered, though, as the relentless tide rose further and her face was finally swamped.

How to go? Should she hold her breath to the very last? Or should she just give herself over gracefully and breathe the river water in right now. Maybe it wouldn't be so bad . . . Her lungs were already hitching and hitching against the lack of oxygen and her heart felt as if it would explode through her rib cage. She could hear it beating faster and faster in her flooded ears. The water was churning—was she kicking and flailing? She didn't even know what her limbs were doing now. She screamed out a torrent of bubbles and prepared to draw death deep down inside her.

As black stars began to frame her vision, warm hands clasped the sides of her face and pulled her up to the surface . . . *almost* the surface. She could see a face, just beyond the thin skin of water which separated her from the air above. A face contorted with panic, shouting, staring. She stared back, unable to make a sound, unable to breathe, unable to escape drowning even in the arms of her rescuer. The chains were holding her firmly under. She was gazing at the life she must leave through the eddying pane of a watery window. It was hard.

Thank you, Michael, she sent, hoping he'd hear it. *But you can't save me. Better let me go.*

Michael pushed his face into the water and kissed her. He sealed his mouth around hers and blew oxygen into her. It was warm and peculiar and her lungs sucked it in like a reflex. Michael pulled away and took in a lungful from above and then returned to breathe into her again. She greedily took it in and the black stars retreated from her vision. But she was still stuck here and he couldn't breathe for her for ever. Not until the tide fell again. It was the kindest thing anyone had done for her . . . but it was going to be one long kiss goodbye.

Michael dragged in as big a lungful of air as he could before plunging back into the water to breathe it into Lisa. His mind was spinning with panic and desperation. He knew this could not go on—how was he to breathe for her and rescue her at the same time? He needed help! Actual, physical help. The spirit world couldn't offer that.

As he pulled up from his fifth exhalation he realized he was beginning to lose full consciousness.

He was seeing things. An otter had just swum in and turned into a dark-haired boy who yelled 'KEEP GOING!' before changing back into an otter and disappearing under the churning dark liquid.

Michael went under again, finding Lisa still gazing at him through the thin membrane which separated her from life and death, her eyes wide and pleading as the last few bubbles of air he'd lent her escaped her mouth. Oh God, this was awful. Dizziness swept him. He was going to fall apart any minute and she would drown. He tried again to untangle the chains that held her down, but the drowned body next to her was hopelessly entangled in them and he had no chance of freeing her.

The otter swam past with something shiny in its mouth. The hallucination shook drops off its fine whiskers in the dimming light from the torch on the walkway and when it turned back into a boy Michael fully expected to pass out.

'KEEP GOING!' yelled the boy. 'I'm going to try this!' He was holding a key.

Michael sucked in another lungful, his eyes stretching with amazement. A spirit? A shapeshifting spirit which could use a key?

The boy ducked under the water and Lisa's body

snagged down deeper into it a second later as her wrists were pulled. Michael dropped in with her and breathed into her mouth again, but she seemed to be pulling in his breath less eagerly now. Her eyes had closed. She was slipping away.

He was shouting with dismay when his head rose again, and a wretchedness settled in his throat and chest, making him want to cry like a child. This was too much. *Too much.*

A sudden shove beneath her sent Lisa high above the water, gasping and croaking and retching. The dark-haired boy had his arms around her and was propelling her up towards Michael. Michael, hanging on to the steady edge of the walkway, reached down and pulled her onto the pontoon and then, with help from the boy, Lisa was hauled up, at last, free of the water as the metal cuffs slid off. They got her up onto the walkway next to the torch. She rolled over onto her front and threw up half a pint of River Thames.

'Where d-did you come from?' Michael peered at the boy as he pulled Lisa's chilled body towards him, and began to rub her arms and shoulders, trying to warm her.

'Cumbria,' said the boy, also shuddering with

184

exhaustion and abating horror. He pushed the straggles of soaked hair off her face. 'Lisa! Lisa! Talk to me!'

Lisa slumped against Michael's chest and turned her pale face up to the boy's. 'You took your time,' she mumbled.

The boy began to laugh. Shocked, slightly hysterical laughter. 'You're still yourself then,' he grinned, shakily. He pulled a bar of chocolate out of his soaked jeans pocket, shook the drops off the plastic wrapper, and opened it. He shared it with them and made them eat their third even though they felt too shocked to even imagine it. 'You need it,' he said.

The chocolate revived her, but Lisa needed the warmth more. Michael had helped but Dax, it turned out, could help better.

'Go furry for me, will you?' she murmured. Michael shouted out with shock as the boy shifted, in the blink of an eye, this time to the shape of a handsome young red fox. Lisa put her arms around the creature and took warmth from it, resting her cheek between its ears and closing her eyes. After five minutes like this, she sat up and blinked and took a sharp breath. 'OK, much better now, thanks.'

Dax shifted back and still had the fox-like grin on his face when he was a boy again. Lisa raised an eyebrow at him. 'In your *dreams,* Jones!' she said. 'I cuddle you strictly in life and death situations.'

He laughed and stood up. 'Control will be freaking out by now. So will Mia and Gideon. We'd better call in and get Chambers to send someone. You can tell me about the dead guy later.'

Lisa stood, allowing a dazed Michael to support her. Her rescuers had revived her remarkably. Even so, she wanted nothing more than to sleep. But that wasn't happening any time soon.

'Wait,' she sighed. 'We're not done yet.'

16

Edwina knew the game was almost over. The police had arrived, along with shoals of press photographers and reporters, only a few minutes after Anton had left. How they knew about this location, she had no idea—but there was a good chance they had seized Anton and were working on him for information. Without result, she was certain. He was made of steel. She knew he would not talk.

If they knew the block but not the exact flat, she still had a few minutes to work out her game plan. She peered carefully through the chink in a torn red curtain in the lounge and cursed as she spotted three Trojans manoeuvring along the narrow road towards the block car park. Armed police *already*? She had been hoping for an ordinary squad car or two, tidying the public out of the way and setting up a cordon while the CO19 crew went through their entry plan back at base.

When the chopper flew overhead and white light began to sweep across the windows on both sides of the poky little flat, Peter panicked and shot someone through the kitchen window. The man was a lunatic but this gave her an idea—something which just might buy her a way out when rescue came for Stacey.

She sidled into the kitchen and saw the idiot crouched by the window. 'Peter! What are you doing?' she hissed, as if she was angry, when in fact she was delighted. As soon as he turned round, fear etched across his bristly face, she sprang across and wrestled the pistol from him. He hissed something in Russian as he gave it up but she didn't bother to translate. She just checked the gun was still loaded, stepped back, and shot him in the head.

He hit the sticky vinyl flooring like a sack of wet sand.

Dropping to the rolled carpet, she struck herself in the face with the barrel of the gun before throwing it on the floor. The blood that sprang from her nose was just the job. Very good. She raked a hand through her hair too, for good measure, making the wiry thatch of it stand up as if it had been pulled. She reached in to the top of the rolled-up carpet and found that Stacey was breathing but still unconscious. She glanced at the gun on the floor and considered. So much better to tie up this loose end while she still could. She tugged the carpet, rolling Stacey over and round onto her front again, loosening it off. Then she backed away towards the window, clambering over Peter's cooling body, keeping low. She reached over and picked up the gun. The angle needed to be right.

Stacey shot out of her stupor. She'd been drowsing through such weird dreams . . . dreams of black water and rats, that odd girl from Harvey Nichols, Edwina being some kind of super-villain. Now she felt a bizarre sense of motion, as if she was being rolled down a slope . . . wrapped up in . . .

'*Carpet!*' she murmured aloud. A smelly old rug of some kind was right in her face, pressing against her nose and brow as she slid and rolled. 'What?' she murmured. 'Wassgoingon?'

She heard someone curse nearby. She tried to sit up but her elbows were still held tight to her body by the partly rolled-up carpet. Was this some kind of game? There was a crunching as she shifted her weight. Like broken glass or china. Then she turned her head and saw Edwina crouching by the far wall of this dingy room she was in. A kitchen? Yes, with a sticky vinyl floor. Shards of glass glittered dimly across it.

'Edwina?' she croaked. 'Eddie?' And then, in a second, it all crashed back through her mind—the insistent white cloth pushing her into sleep, being shackled to the pontoon by the dark water, Edwina ordering her around with that awful man helping her . . . and Lisa. Lisa left behind and probably murdered.

'Don't make a noise, princess,' said Edwina and now, through bleary eyes, Stacey saw that her former minder was training a gun on her. It was quite surreal—and for a few moments she genuinely believed it had to be a dream. But then the filthy stench of the carpet and scrape of its cheap backing against her hands cut through and she knew—*had* to know—that this was real. Surges of fear and fury began pounding through her.

'You conniving, backstabbing lowlife,' she spat— and then repeated it in Russian for good measure. Curses always sounded better in Russian.

'Whatever you say next will be your last word,' warned Edwina, glancing up at the shattered window while levelling the gun at her head. So Stacey contented herself with glaring at the woman with utter disdain. It was better than focusing on the body in front of her and the widening pool of port-red blood beneath it.

She began to wriggle, desperate to be free. If she had to be shot it would be better while she was making a run for it—not trussed up like a Christmas turkey. Her heritage pulsed furiously through her. None of her ancestors would have tolerated such an end without a fight. There was flashing light and a thudding noise outside the window which was distracting Edwina, making her eyes flicker to the side. She had a calculating look on her face as she glanced through the smashed opening and then back at the gun. And in the time it took to do this Stacey rolled and got one arm free.

'Go for it,' said Edwina, much to her surprise. 'I'll get a better shot when you're clear of all that cheap shag pile.'

Stacey grabbed a large triangular shard of glass and held it up as she struggled to a sitting position.

Edwina laughed. 'You can try,' she snorted. 'Go

on—I'll give you a two second start. You might dent my knee before you die. You should know I never miss. *Never.'*

Stacey did not lunge forward but she tilted the glass in her hand, testing its weight and shape. She curled her hand in at the wrist and fixed her haughtiest stare on Edwina's face.

And frisbee'd the glass right into her neck.

Edwina made a choking noise and pulled the trigger. And Stacey crashed backwards onto the kitchen floor amid a cloud of dust and glass splinters, her eyes rolling up into her head.

When the entry team kicked the door in and moved expertly into the flat, pistols scanning the air like stubby black antennae, they found the missing girl in the arms of her female minder, whose nose and throat were bleeding profusely. Through their shouts of '*DOWN! DOWN! GET DOWN!*' the sobbing woman pointed to the dead man a few feet away. 'He's killed her. Oh God, he's killed her! S-Stacey tried to get him with the glass, but he—he shot her. And then I—went for him and got the gun and I sh-shot him! Oh God . . . my poor Stacey.'

The armed officer kept his gun on her and nodded to a colleague to check the girl. The man pulled the limp body away from the hysterical woman and noticed right away that her eyes were open. And blinking.

'Can you speak?' he urged, his expert eye taking in the graze wound of a bullet on her left temple. She did not reply as she lapsed back into unconsciousness.

'There's nothing like a bit of frock shopping to take your mind off an afternoon spent floating with a corpse,' said Lisa.

At about the time Dax Jones, back in falcon form, was dropping into the park beside the Sadler's Wells Theatre and finding a roost in a tree, Lisa was also heading for her spiritual home. She and Michael ran into *DRESS/IMPRESS,* a posh frocks boutique just a few streets away, having abandoned the Triumph in a motorbike bay around the corner.

The sales assistant, in a sleek black trouser suit and oversized pearls, curled her lip at the teenager, barefoot in a soaked sweatshirt and tracksuit bottoms. She was about to stride over and ask her to leave the premises when she glanced at the man beside the girl and her thickly-lipsticked mouth fell open. 'Oh!' she gasped. 'You're Michael O'Flanagan! I *love* your thing on *The T Show*!'

'Great!' beamed Michael, twinkling with every ounce of Irish charm he could muster in his exhausted, anxious state. 'Then you'll want to help me! We're in a *huge* rush—I've got to get this girl into a decent frock and across to the red carpet at Sadler's Wells in about ten minutes. Can you help us?'

He pulled out a gold credit card from his jacket pocket in case the sales assistant had any second thoughts. He needn't have worried. She was already running her practised eye up and down Lisa's damp form and reaching for a rail of glossy dresses. 'Size eight, yes?' she guessed, correctly. Lisa nodded. 'Blonde, when dry?' The sales assistant picked up a lock of damp hair with a wince. Lisa nodded again.

'Shoe size?' The assistant went to a rack of sparkly sandals.

'Five,' said Lisa. 'But can't do a very high heel. May have to run for my life.'

'O-K, this is the one for you,' said the sales assistant, with total confidence which, if there had only been time, Lisa would have had great respect for. She loved a high fashion sales assistant who knew her stuff.

In the changing room she peeled off the disgusting tracksuit bottoms and top, and gratefully received the fluffy white towel that arrived over the top of the door. The dress was a shimmering blue sheath which hung to mid-calf length, with exquisite crystal beading around the halter neck. It slid across her skin like silk; a wonderful balm after the horrors her poor body had experienced over the past few hours. The diamante sandals were also a perfect fit and the heels were modest—run-able.

As she stepped back outside Michael let out a low whistle which was immediately drowned out by the assistant advancing with a gusting hair drier and brush.

'We don't really have time for this.' Michael checked his watch, edgily. 'Not if you're right about Stacey's father.'

Lisa eyed him frostily. 'I am NOT going onto the red carpet in front of the world's press with half the River Thames in my hair. Two minutes, Mystic!'

The sales assistant expertly dried and brushed Lisa's hair into a softly folded loop, securing it neatly at the nape of her neck with an oval glittery clip. Lisa glanced in the mirror and nodded with approval. 'I'm coming back here,' she said to the woman, who raised an uncertain eyebrow in response. 'Don't worry,' she added. 'I'm very rich and stylish in my own time. I'm only helping out Mr Charm over there after he got me dropped in the river.'

'O-K,' said the woman, again, and clipped some costume sapphire earrings to Lisa's earlobes.

'No make-up,' winced Lisa.

'You don't need it,' sighed the woman with an envious shrug. But she supplied some mascara and lip gloss as if by magic and Lisa deftly applied both in thirty seconds while Michael paid with his gold card, tapping in his pin number at great speed.

Hey, get over yourself, you vain tart, Sylv interrupted, back now with a proper level of energy. *Time to go!*

'Are you sure they'll let us through?' asked Lisa, as they hurried towards a crowd of press and onlookers, a seething mass of anticipation under spotlights around the theatre.

Michael pulled a gilt-edged white card, folded in half, from his jacket pocket. It was his invitation to the Bolshoi Ballet's performance of *Swan Lake*—in aid of some global charity. It wasn't really his kind of thing, but his agent had insisted he attend for the publicity. 'They'll let us through,' he said, grasping her hand.

'Even in the state you're in?' she asked, feeling rather smug at how good *she* looked.

'Look—I'm a psychic medium. I'm not meant to look like a politician,' he said, dragging her to the burly suited men at the edge of the red carpet. 'So, my trousers are worryingly damp and my poor boots look like something from the *Titanic*—but this jacket cost a fortune. I'm . . . bohemian. It's allowed.'

As if in agreement, a crowd of females some way behind the cordon started squealing, 'Michael! Michael! Oh, Mystic Mike!'

'Good to see you, sir,' said one of the burly men, taking the invitation and smiling at Lisa. 'And this is?'

'My plus one,' said Michael with a head tilt and a grin. 'Can't say who—it'd be all over the papers tomorrow morning!'

Lisa just smirked and they were allowed past onto the red carpet, in the wake of . . . um . . . yes, that was definitely Sting. And—oh—yep, Elton John, Lisa realized. She couldn't wait to tell Mia.

Sleek black limousines endlessly rolled along the approach to the theatre, depositing a stream of VIPs beside the security cordon at the foot of the red carpet. Lisa and Michael loitered near to it, watching the arrivals.

'Are they here yet, either of them?' asked Michael. His fingers were hot in hers. She let them go.

'No. Soon, though. Very soon.'

'Mike! Mike! Mike's lady friend—over here!' yelled a man, and then a barrage of flashes went off as they turned. Of course. The press.

'Pose,' said Michael, taking her hand again. 'Go on—you know you were born to it!'

Lisa did pose. She threw back her head and laughed and she dropped her chin and pouted, and put one hand on an angled hip, showing the fabulous blue dress off to its best advantage. She *was* enjoying it, but there was another reason for playing up to all the attention. They couldn't go into the theatre yet. They *had* to stay on the red carpet. Sylv was insisting on it and once again telling her: *Top dog. Red carpet. Bolshy. Sharp diamond.*

Top dog—they had already decided who that was. Who was the top dog in Britain if not the Prime Minister? Michael knew he was to be attending tonight—they'd worked that out while they were leaving the boathouse and running for the bike. By the time Lisa was strapping on the helmet and getting on behind Michael, Sylv had agreed. Yes. Top dog was the PM. And bolshy was the Bolshoi and the Bolshoi Ballet performance was here, at the Sadler's Wells—the very event Michael had been invited to weeks ago. And here they were on the red carpet, waiting. Who said the other side didn't plan in advance?

'So—Stacey's father has agreed to do something to the PM,' said Lisa, still posing and talking across to Michael amid the hubbub. 'But maybe he knows she's safe by now—so maybe he's not going to come?'

'Maybe,' agreed Michael. 'I'm pretty certain he won't be coming when he knows Stacey is alive and safe. And I think she is . . . But does he know that? He told the police she was at home with him when she wasn't, so he must have decided to do as he was told after the kidnappers called him. I'm betting he blocked all other calls except theirs.'

'Well, if he shows up we'll know, won't we?' said Lisa. But it was getting hard to stay put and find out. The paps had turned their attention to a glamorous young actress and her rock star boyfriend, walking up behind them.

'Don't think we can milk this much longer,' said Michael, grinning and talking through his teeth. 'When will your PM get here?'

'About . . . now,' muttered Lisa, peering past the celebrity couple as another limousine passed. 'Here's our man.'

Blocking their view, a suited security man came up to gently usher them along towards the theatre. '*Damn!*' cursed Michael, under his breath, trying to keep his eyes locked on the man getting out of the limo. Yes—Lisa was right. The British Prime Minister was smiling broadly at the public and straightening his tie. Flanked by security, surely no crazed killer could get at him?

No. But a well known and well liked ambassador friend certainly could.

'Oh no!' squeaked Lisa, suddenly plucking oddly at her eyeball. 'Oh no! I've lost my contact lens.'

She dropped to her knees and pretended to search the red carpet. Michael joined her and the security guard sighed and stepped back, allowing them a little more time. A few cameras flashed in their direction. This would probably make the

Heat magazine 'funny things the stars do' section.

Further down the carpet the PM was beginning to move towards them, slowly, suited minders trailing him to the left and right and his wife, pretty in pink, at his side.

Now another limo pulled up and from it climbed a tall man with a straight back, a fine greying beard and very dark eyes. Lisa stared at Volkov. So this was Stacey's father. She recognized him from the images she'd rummaged through in Stacey's mind. *Help me read him, Sylv,* she asked. The man was smiling at the security cordon crew and being ushered through. He gave a little wave to the crowd and then dropped his gaze to his hands. He was no celebrity and got little paparazzi attention.

His hands, said Sylv. *Hands.*

Something tickled in Lisa's memory. Her conversation with Stacey in the dark of the boatshed. What had she said about her father's hands? *Aloe vera, chamomile and tea tree oil.* The memory came back in slivers as she went on pretending to hunt for her lens on the red carpet. *Hates a gripping handshake . . .*

'Is that him? I think it is!' hissed Michael, his head close to hers so his hair brushed her cheek.

'What are we to do? Will I just go and rugby tackle him? What if he's got a bomb under his tux?'

'Ssshh! Let me concentrate.' She rose to her knees and he helped her back up to her feet. They stepped aside and let the celebrity actress/rock star combo pass them, both celebs giving them rather contemptuous glances. It was clearly not the done thing to loiter in somebody else's limelight.

His *hands*. Something was not right with his hands.

The Russian ambassador moved towards the Prime Minister who had turned to greet him. Lisa could see that the smile on Volkov's face was waxy—set like a mask. Whatever he was about to do, it was soon. His expression was resolute and fixed—that of a man who knew his life would soon be over. A bomb? No! No—it was not that. *Help me read him, Sylv!* she called again but Sylv said only two words and precisely as she said them Lisa knew what was wrong.

'Ring! He has a ring on!' She clutched Michael's arm in sudden, horrified realization. 'He can't wear rings—his skin erupts. But he has one on!'

She began to run towards the Prime Minister, yelling out: 'STOP! STOP HIM! DON'T SHAKE HIS HAND!'

The reaction from the PM's minders was instant. Lisa was on the floor three seconds later, grabbed by two men while a flurry of excitement and a few screams rebounded around the crowd.

'DON'T LET THE PRIME MINISTER SHAKE HIS HAND!' Lisa shrieked, elbowing one of the men hard in the chest. 'THE RING! IT'S POISONED! *SHARP DIAMOND!*'

Michael was shouting behind her too, and also being manhandled away, but in all the hubbub, Lisa could not make herself heard and between the knees of one of the bodyguards she could see the Prime Minister shrugging in a 'no big deal' kind of way for the cameras and turning back to the ambassador.

'NOOOOOOOOOOO!' she screamed again. Her scream was cut off as one of the men put a large hand across her mouth, chiding, 'Now stop it! Behave yourself!'

She was roughly flipped over onto her front and twisted her head round just in time to see the glint of the gold and diamond ring—the sharp point of the jewel turned inward—on Volvok's right hand as it went to clasp the hand of the Prime Minister. The poison in the diamond would travel down the sharp point on impact, like ink down a nib, and kill the PM inside twenty seconds. This nasty piece of information was floating around Volkov's head like a grey shroud. Lisa groaned and shut her eyes. She didn't want to see another death today.

The next second there was another loud scream—this time from the Prime Minister's wife. Lisa's eyes sprang open again in time to see a feathered missile plummet between the two men and strike the forearm of the Russian. Wings beat, talons flailed. The Russian staggered backwards. More astonished yelps and cries rose up in the air and the flashbulbs went into a frenzy. A female TV commentator's voice cut through: 'And it seems as if the PM, or maybe the Russian ambassador, has been attacked . . . by a—you'll never believe this, Sophie—by a FALCON!'

The Russian ambassador was being helped away from the PM, blood dripping from his wrist and a dazed expression on his face. He was moving closer to Lisa and Michael, surrounded by yet more body-guards. Now he was looking at the ring and there was a terrible intent on his face. He knew the plan had failed. He believed his daughter was about to die. He was considering using the sharp dia-mond on himself. Lisa tried to shout but she heard

Michael call out above her head. 'Mr Volkov! It's OK! Stacey is SAFE! Nastya is SAFE! It's OK! It's all over! Don't touch the ring! Don't!'

'And the falcon . . . a peregrine, if my bird knowledge serves, is circling above us . . . can you get that? Can you get it on camera, Phil?' The TV reporter squinted up into the evening light. 'Do you think it might be going to attack again? Have we disturbed a nest or something?' she babbled. 'Oh—wow—did you see that? I've never seen a bird move so fast! It's gone now. Completely out of sight . . . and the PM seems to be fine—he's laughing and dusting some feathers off—and the Russian ambassador is getting some medical attention. What with crazed hawks and that protest of some sort from the young lady with Mystic Michael O'Flanagan, I'm betting people are going to remember this charity ballet mostly for what went on *outside* the theatre! What a night! Back to you in the studio . . .'

17

'Just two things, please,' said Lisa, with her sweetest smile. The Prime Minister smiled back, one eyebrow raised in anticipation, and Lisa flicked a glance at David Chambers, the head of the Cola Project, who had, in the past twenty-four hours, co-ordinated everything from Stacey's rescue to the team of government operatives which had efficiently swooped on the red carpet event as soon as the drama of last night's attempted assassination unfolded.

'Go on,' prompted the PM, sitting back in his leather armchair. He looked like a kindly uncle— as well he might, given that this 'niece', with a little help from her friends, had recently saved him from death by poisoning.

'First, I would like to speak to Michael O' Flanagan again, before we have to go,' said Lisa.

'This is the psychic medium chap—the TV one, yes?' asked the Prime Minister, still managing to look sceptical even though he'd been informed that what Michael and Lisa had done to save him was largely thanks to their combined psychic medium talents.

'Yes, the TV one,' agreed Lisa, with a little wince of embarrassment. She did not, for one second, want this man, or Chambers, to think she was one of Michael's thousands of adoring fans. *Eeeugh*. 'I owe him some thankyous, for what he did for me.'

Chambers shifted in his chair, ill at ease.

'Look—I know you won't let me see him again, Mr Chambers, once we're back in Fenton Lodge. I doubt you'll let me out for a decade! Or Mia. Or Dax. Even though none of this was our fault *and* we saved lives!'

'Dax?' enquired the PM, looking perplexed.

'The falcon that attacked Volkov,' explained Chambers, twirling a silver ballpoint through his fingers. 'It was one of our Colas. The shapeshifter boy, Dax Jones.'

'Aaah—Dax Jones,' murmured the PM, stroking his chin and nodding. 'Astonishing!'

'Yes,' said Chambers drily. 'And an outrageous breach of Cola security rules.'

'But . . . in the circumstances,' nodded the PM, 'perhaps you could go easy on him. After all . . . isn't that what our most valuable assets are for? The greater good of the country.'

Chambers compressed his lips and nodded. He gave his silver pen one solitary click and put it back in his jacket pocket.

'*Any*way,' Lisa persisted, 'I know that seeing him again is unlikely. So before we go back, can I? He's quite safe, you know. He saved my life! And Stacey's. You guys would never have got there in time if you hadn't followed the tip-offs from all those press photographers he got so excited, would you?' she added, glaring at Chambers.

'We had some help from Mia, too,' said Chambers. 'But yes, O'Flanagan led us there, in a very cack-handed fashion.'

'And how is Stacey, by the way?' said Lisa in an offhand way which didn't quite convince Chambers, who knew her too well.

'She's recovering well,' he said. 'Her father is with her and he's recovering from the ordeal he went through too.'

'*His* ordeal?' snorted the Prime Minister. '*I* was the one he nearly killed!' Then he smiled and shook his head. 'It's a peculiar thing when someone tries to kill you and you find yourself fighting all due process to make sure he's not arrested and locked away for life.'

Lisa glanced up at him. 'You're letting him go?'

'In a manner of speaking,' said the PM. 'Very few people know the facts and Volkov was an excellent contact for us. Taking action against him would be pointless and only playing into the hands of the people who tried to have me killed. They want disharmony between the UK and Russia and I'm not willing to hand it to them on a plate. No . . . Volkov is "retiring" to spend more time with his daughter. He'll be leaving the country, of course. And never speaking of the last twenty-four hours to anyone.'

'Which brings me to your Irishman,' said Chambers. 'He knows far too much about you, Lisa. And Mia. And Dax.'

'He's a psychic,' shrugged Lisa. 'I couldn't stop him getting into our heads.'

Chambers looked very sceptical.

'And we all owe him!' insisted Lisa. 'And you know he's all right!'

'He checks out OK,' said Chambers, who had

debriefed the young Irishman himself and found that he rather liked him. 'He'll have to sign the Official Secrets Act, of course, and he'll be a "person of interest" to us for ever now. But . . . I don't think he plans to cause us any problems.'

'Then you shall see him,' said the PM. 'And your second desire, Miss Hardman?' He smiled again, clearly finding it all rather amusing.

Lisa put her china teacup into its saucer on the edge of the PM's huge walnut desk and fixed him with her dark blue gaze. 'Since I got to London I've had surveillance, ghosts, stuck-up Russian heiresses, cabaret act mediums, half murdered MI5 agents, psycho minders turned bad, dead dogs, dead terrorists, *really* nasty clothes and a seriously bad hair day. Prime Minister, after all this, even though Mr Chambers here is desperate to get me back up to Fenton Lodge and barricade me in . . . don't you think I deserve just *one day* of proper *shopping?*'

The PM stared at her for a moment and then back at Chambers. He consulted his watch. It was still early; only 9.15 a.m. 'Chambers,' he said. 'you can get the rest of the debriefing done when you're safely back in Cumbria—tomorrow. Get her

a meeting with O'Flanagan by 10.30. And then . . . '
he glanced back at Lisa and chuckled, 'she shops
till she drops.'

Mia gave her a long hug when they returned to
the hotel, sending waves of warmth and comfort.
'Chambers told me what had happened to you.
Oh, Lees—I should never have let you go off like
that! I had no idea what you were getting into. I
could hardly sleep last night.'

Lisa squeezed her back and then pushed her
friend away before Mia could pick up the earth-
quake of emotions inside her.

'It was OK in the end, though. Michael and Dax
saved me.'

'But . . . to be stuck in the water with a floating
corpse . . . for ages . . . ' Mia shuddered.

'I'm fine,' murmured Lisa as they headed into
the lift, two brand new MI5 minders just behind
them. 'And I've got us a bit more shopping time!'

'Sorry?' said Mia, turning round as the lift doors
closed on the four of them, and tilting her head to
one side. 'I can't hear you properly. It hasn't come
back yet.'

Lisa shook her head. 'Look what happens when I leave you alone for five minutes!'

Chambers had told Lisa what Mia had done for the injured Jeff and Gary. Realizing that they might never recover their hearing if left too long as they were, she had laid her hands on both their heads and stayed put, healing in a constant flow until the ambulances arrived. At the same time she had held the onlookers at bay by sending them all surges of 'Mia Effect' that made them adore her so much they didn't interfere, bringing blankets and water and other useful things instead, for the half hour it took before the first ambulance made it through the traffic to the store. By then Gary's and Jeff's inner ear machinery was all fixed. And Mia was completely deaf.

'I feel so bad. I let you down,' said Mia, with a gulp. 'I couldn't hear anything. It was so weird. I couldn't have a phone conversation with Control so I sent them a text about Gary and Jeff—and that I was going to the hotel and they needed to meet me there. Someone got me a taxi and I went back, thinking you'd be there too before long. And then I just sort of . . . conked out in my room until some new minders burst in and everything went all Cola

Project deadly serious.'

'It wouldn't have made any difference, so stop beating yourself up,' said Lisa, loudly.

'It was a good thing Michael had started making a public nuisance of himself,' said Mia. 'Control tracked him down through the press and sent in their own unit to get Stacey. They thought you were with her, you see. It was all about you, really.'

The lift pinged at their floor and they stepped out, minders in tow, to find Chambers striding up the thickly carpeted corridor towards them.

'OK, Lisa. Your wish is the PM's command. The TV medium's here. Come with me now. You've got half an hour. That's all.'

Mia turned to stare at her. 'He's here? Michael?' She gave her friend an appraising glance and added, 'So that's what all the quaking is about!'

'What quaking?' snapped Lisa. 'I'm fine!'

Mia smiled. 'And your favourite T-shirt and jeans.'

Lisa tossed her hair, washed and conditioned to a silky finish once again, and glanced in a passing wall mirror at the pale blue top and sleek indigo jeans, with a chain belt of silver-dipped shells. She had been trying to convince herself that it was all for the Prime Minister, but Mia clearly wasn't fooled.

Chambers steered her back to the lift and they went up to the top floor—the roof garden of the hotel. As the door slid back they stepped out under an archway of pink roses. On either side of it were the incongruous shapes of two more armed MI5 operatives. The roof garden had been thoroughly checked and cleared before Michael had been allowed up. He stood now, at the far end, leaning over a wrought-iron Victorian balustrade and gazing at the city below.

Lisa stepped across the gravel path that wound around a small circular lawn with an ornamental pond and fountain at the centre. Past the potted bay trees, sculpted into orbs, and the banks of pretty floral shrubs in planters, she made for a wooden arbour, festooned with honeysuckle, at the far end of the roof garden. She settled into it, inhaling the pine and honey scent and staring at the side of Michael's head. He had not looked round. He was also wearing fresh clothes: a brown leather jacket and blue jeans tucked into more sharp-toed townie boots. His dark hair wafted about in the breeze. He looked ridiculous. In a handsome, squeamishly romantic way. She could see why he got legions of doe-eyed fans.

Eventually she sent *OK, Two Star, I'm here . . .* and immediately he turned round and stared across at her.

'More like three star now, I think,' he said as he approached her.

'Well, *yeah*! You just picked up my telepathic message! No problem.' She smiled at him, impressed and pleased, as he sat down beside her.

'How are *you* then, Seven Star?'

'Fine,' she said.

'Yeah. Right.' His leather jacket creaked as he settled back next to her under the wooden hood of the arbour.

'What would you know?' she challenged and then drew a sharp breath as he put his arm round her shoulders and pulled her towards him. 'Don't start getting ideas, O'Flanagan!' she squeaked, her heart thumping.

'Ideas? Well . . . let's see . . . ' He closed his eyes and she realized, with surprise, that he was reading her. Her first instinct was to pull away and shut everything down. Damn *liberty*! But something in her over-rode that and gave in. He might as well know. She would never see him again after today anyway. She unclenched her fists and noticed, with a small thrum in her ribcage, how he smelt of warm skin and leather and soap.

After a long pause he said, 'It's no fun being you, is it?'

'Well . . . ' She tried to laugh, suddenly dry of mouth. 'It has its moments.'

'Nobody knows, do they?' He released his grip so he could turn to look at her and his eyes swam with . . . what was that? Pity?

She said nothing. Could think of nothing. Just watched her own face in his eyes and breathed in. And out. In again.

'You've never really let anyone see, have you? The full extent of it . . . The endless . . . God, the queues! The shouting. The crying . . . whispering . . . ' he went on. He glanced back at Chambers and the operatives on the far side of the roof. 'They don't know. Not even Mia . . . '

'Rubbish. They know. I complain all the time.' She grinned, and almost heard the crack her face made.

'Maybe, but that's not the same.'

'Nobody *can* know,' she said, clasping her hands and weaving her fingers tightly. 'You kind of have to be there. And actually, I wouldn't wish it on anyone.'

'Wish it on me.'

She stared at him. 'Are you serious? After what you've just said? Do you *really* want to see any more of what goes on in my head?'

'I want to share it. I want you to have one person in this world who understands,' he said, and she saw then that his hands were shaking and his jaw was set. He was not on an ego trip. He meant what he said. And what would that be like? Would it help to let him see?

'Well?' His eyes were locked on hers and his hands were on her shoulders. He was waiting at the doors of Lisa Hell. Did he deserve to come in? She felt a twinge of sorrow for him because suddenly she knew—she was going to let him. She rode the wave of her decision and leaned across, put her hand to his cheek and kissed his mouth. It was shocking and wonderful at the same time. He jumped, startled, and then kissed her back . . . just a little . . . and one hand touched the back of her head lightly. Although her heart was thundering with astonishment at its own audacious decision she ordered it to relax, go into freefall, as Michael began to read her mind and soul.

Images flooded in: spirits she had helped, spirits she had ignored, lost things she had found . . . lost people she had found too late . . . Sylv's presence, strong and caring . . . the drift of calmer beings who only observed and occasionally offered guidance and random observations . . . the unruly queue of desperate souls clamouring for action . . . the children, the elderly, even animals . . . death scene upon death scene . . . the occasional fleeting glimmer of truly evil entities which sought to reach and use her . . . something grey and snarling; a man with white hair and icy blue eyes on a darkening beach . . . a whirling, shrieking, talking, singing, weeping, sighing, insidious and insistent maelstrom that never ended . . . Lisa was separated from it by such a thin shutter, shored up by Sylv on the spirit side and her friends here among the living. Mia, Gideon, and most of all that boy/fox/falcon/otter creature called Dax. Without them how would she be? *You know how I would be,* she told him. *If that shutter ever buckles I will be insane within a week. Don't believe me? Ah . . . I see you do.*

When she felt his tears on her face she gently pushed him back out of her mind. She waited until his sense of place returned before she finished the kiss, though. It was lovely to kiss him and she did not want to break it off while he was still horror-struck.

At last his eyes opened and, running his thumb softly across her lower lip, he regretfully drew away. He said nothing for quite some time, scrubbing away the tears and staring out across the rooftops of the city until his hitching chest had evened out and his shaking had eased a little.

'I'm sorry,' said Lisa. 'I should have said no.'

'No . . . I insisted,' he gulped, not looking at her. 'And . . . dear God, I'm sorry too. I—I don't know how you go on, so.'

She shrugged. 'You get used to it. You learn ways to cope.'

'Like being a smart mouthed, bolshy little madam,' he grinned, allowing a chuckle out.

'That's me!'

'Got to go, Lisa!' Chambers called from the other side of the roof and she realized, with amazement, that the bitter-sweet kiss must have lasted for minutes on end.

Michael stood up and turned to her. 'I will never forget you,' he said.

She smiled, sadly. 'Ah well, try to remember me in the blue dress, will you? Not in the soggy track-suit bottoms. Just edit those out.'

He pulled her to him and gave her a hug. 'I

mean, I will think of you every day,' he said, his breath warm on the top of her head. 'And if you ever leave the Cola college or whatever it is, and need someone . . . you find me, OK? Find *me*.'

She nodded and stepped away reluctantly as Chambers approached. She would never see him again. Unless she tuned into *The T Show*, of course. And she might do that.

'Time to go,' said Chambers. There was compassion in his voice, mixed with the caution and the warning.

Michael nodded and shook his hand. 'Look after her,' he said.

18

'You have *got* to look at these!' Mia clambered into the armoured 4x4 with an armful of newspapers from the service station WHSmith's.

Lisa shoved the pile of shiny, sparkly shopping bags to one side of the wide leather bench seat and took the papers.

'Great work, Lisa,' said Chambers drily, from the front passenger seat. He had papers on his knee too as the driver pulled away and even the silent MI5 operatives in the back of the vehicle were snorting with amusement at the headlines.

MYSTIC MIKE SAVES KIDNAPPED TEEN

screamed the *Sun* and a strap line below it read

AND OUR BRAVE SNAPPER TAKES A BULLET!

Inside was an over-excited story almost entirely but not quite unlike the real one.

TELLY psychic Michael O'Flanagan called on the *Sun* to help when his spirit guide warned that 15-year-old Stacey Volkova, daughter of the Russian Ambassador, was kidnapped in an extortion plot.

And our own photographer, Jason Harris, took him on a mercy dash across the city to the kidnapper's lair, only to be shot by one of the mob as he tried to help with the rescue.

When he could not convince the cops to believe him, Mystic Mike took action on his own.

'I had to do something because nobody was taking me seriously,' said Mike, exclusively to the *Sun*.

'Stacey is one of my clients and my spirit guide, Sean, told me she was in trouble while I was in the middle of a signing session for my book—*Through My Eyes* (BarkerCollier £14.99)—at Harvey Nichols.

'I knew that I had to do something, even though the police thought I was just pulling a publicity stunt. That's when Jason came to my aid and together, on his motorbike, we tracked down Stacey in a Tower Hamlets flat—and incapacitated one of the thugs who'd taken her.'

Lisa read on, shaking her head. 'So—where am *I* in all this?'

'Exactly where you should be,' said Chambers from the front seat. 'Nowhere! The only thing *you* did, yesterday, was try to shout some half-baked teen-age protest at the Prime Minister outside Sadler's Wells. You're on page nine if you must see it.'

And there she was, in the gorgeous blue dress, posing like a starlet in one shot, and sprawling on the floor like a lunatic in the next one.

UNKNOWN BLONDE IN
RED CARPET PROTEST

was the headline. Michael was not in any of the photos. Lisa guessed the Cola Project team had gone to work on all the national press editors on that one. She realized she would only ever be 'Unknown Blonde'.

Mia went into fits of laughter at the photos. All the other papers carried reports about Mystic Mike's amazing rescue, but they were vague on the details when it came to the Russian Ambassador and his daughter.

'So, what's going to happen to Volkov and Stacey now?' Lisa wondered. 'And did they get all the people involved?'

'Well, at least two of them ended up dead,' said Chambers. 'One you met and did for yourself, if I'm not mistaken, and the other was killed by the woman—Edwina Krantz—we think,' said Chambers. 'The other one, Anton Chapayev, was found unconscious in a utility cupboard at the block of flats where they were holding Stacey. Turns out your Irish hero knocked *him* out.'

Lisa smiled, a warm rush of pride inside her.

'Another man turned up dead in some woodland, along with Stacey's pet dog,' went on Chambers. 'That turned out to be Kris Myers—one of Stacey's minders. Looks as though he was despatched for being too loyal to her father. Edwina Krantz . . . ' he paused and sucked air through his teeth, ' . . . is still at large. She duped the rescue team into believing she had been kidnapped too.' He raised his eyebrows. 'And some cretin allowed her to escape from an ambulance. They'll find her though. And whoever else was behind it all. I'm glad to say that's not my problem.'

'But will Stacey really have to leave the country?' Lisa asked again. 'Seems hard. She'll have to leave all that London shopping . . . ' She felt oddly concerned for the girl; something she was not used to. She rarely concerned herself with anyone outside Dax, Mia, Gideon, and her father.

'Call her if you like,' said Chambers, passing back his mobile with Stacey's number already dialled and ringing. 'She asked to talk to you. Keep it brief, though.'

The phone burred three times before Stacey

picked up. 'Yes? Hello?' she said, eagerly.

'Hi . . . um . . . it's me. Lisa.'

'Lisa! Wow! I can't believe it. Are you OK?'

Lisa laughed. 'I was going to ask you that.'

'You first,' said Stacey. 'I can't believe you got out alive. I felt sure that guy was going to kill you.'

'Well, he did try,' said Lisa, doing her best not to remember the details. 'What happened after that woman took you away?'

'I don't remember very much,' said Stacey. 'Just being trussed up like a chicken in the back of a van one moment and then being wrapped up in a manky carpet the next. Eeeugh. Can you believe that? It wasn't even clean!'

'But you're OK?' prompted Lisa. The girl certainly sounded OK.

'Yes—I think so. I guess it helps that they kept knocking me out,' she said, wryly. 'Although I do remember bits and pieces, they're a bit weird. I keep thinking of playing frisbee with Edwina . . . don't know why. Probably the effect of all that chloroform.'

She tailed off and then added, with a sigh, 'The worst bit was losing Tolstoy.' Lisa felt the girl's sadness buffet at her. 'And, of course, being in that disgusting boatshed with you. And then thinking they were going to kill you. I never did say thanks to you for coming to save me. Thanks . . . you know?'

'You're welcome,' murmured Lisa. 'But Michael probably did more.'

'Oooh. Isn't he gorgeous?' sighed Stacey. 'Wouldn't you just . . . ? If you could. But hey, no chance of that. Dad's taking me to America. He's not in trouble or anything—the Prime Minister is his friend. He understood what happened. So . . . anyway, Dad's just going to leave his job and we're going to travel. And I'll get to spend more time with Mum in LA too. That's good . . . I think. Although I'll have to come back in a year or two to be a model, obviously. All the agencies want me. Or . . . I might work for one of those pet rescue shows on TV. Or with kids in those sports charity things . . . What do you think?'

Chambers made a winding-up action with his hand as Lisa smiled into the phone. 'You'll be a great model,' Lisa said. 'Or a great celebrity pet rescuer. Or superstar sports trainer . . . Or all three. See you in *Heat* magazine some day. Take care.'

'You too!' There was a click and Lisa handed back the phone.

'You were *nice* to her,' marvelled Mia.

Lisa shrugged. 'Well—I'm tired. Not on form.'

Mia smiled and sat back into her corner of the seat, eyeing her friend knowingly.

'You cared,' she said. 'And you cared about Michael too.'

Lisa looked out of the window as the M6 blurred past in the dark. Michael. Two star. Well, actually four star now. She realized that the kiss had been much like putting jump leads between two car engines. She had started something in him and she didn't know if he would thank her for it in the end. He may have started something in her, too.

Another teenage girl was on her mind.

'When we get back,' she said, leaning across to Chambers. 'I have a spirit communication slip to fill in. About a girl who drowned in the Thames in 1871. Her name is Charlotte. There are some things we need to do for her.'

Mia nudged her. 'Vengeance seeker?' she mouthed, looking astonished.

Lisa shook her head. 'No—she just wants the facts laid out properly. To clear someone's name . . . '

'OK,' said Chambers. 'We'll get to her. We're still working through last week's slips, you know.'

'No—this one takes priority,' said Lisa, firmly. She settled back into the seat and took in Mia's amazed look.

'Since when did any spirit get so important to you?' asked Chambers.

'Since yesterday,' Lisa smiled.

'I owe her.'

Ali Sparkes is a journalist and BBC broadcaster who chucked in the safe job to go dangerously freelance and try her hand at writing comedy scripts. Her first venture was as a comedy columnist on *Woman's Hour* and later on *Home Truths*. Not long after, she discovered her real love was writing children's fiction.

Ali grew up adoring adventure stories about kids who mess about in the woods and still likes to mess about in the woods herself whenever possible. She lives with her husband and two sons in Southhampton, England. Check out www.alisparkes.com for the latest news on Ali's forthcoming books.

UNLEASHED

MIND OVER MATTER
OUT NOW!

A tiny avalanche of pebbles tumbled down the cliff face. They rattled musically as they bounced off large chunks of chalk, flint, and Wealden clay.

'Go on,' said Gideon, staring up at the ribbed grey curve of the Best Ammonite In The World. 'Keep going. Left and right . . . ge-e-ently . . .'

Luke nodded and held his sightline as if his pale green eyes were lasers boring into the cliff. And, in a manner of speaking, they were. The ammonite, five or six metres up in the crumbly edifice, nudged a little to the left.

'Keeeeep it coming,' said Gideon, rubbing his hands through his fluffy blond hair in tense concentration. 'As soon as it's out I'll catch it and bring it down safely . . . Yeeees . . . Just a bit further down. A biiiit furthe—*DOOF!*'

CRACK! The impact between his shoulder blades was so sudden and so forceful that the air was knocked out of his lungs and he was smacked face down into the gritty foot of the cliff. He was dimly aware that Luke had executed the same maneouvre and, as he scrambled round to see their attacker, his brother did likewise, a mirror image to his right.

Both of them were hauled up into a standing position and roughly shaken by one shoulder. Only one man held them but they knew better than to attempt to struggle out of the iron grip.

'Wh-what?' squawked Gideon, trying to sound indignant rather than guilty.

It didn't work.

'Try me!' rumbled the heavy-browed man who had them immobilized. 'Just once more.'

'U-Uncle Jem!' Gideon's eyes skittered around, trying to remind the man that the beach had people on it. *Normal* people. Admittedly, probably only about two dozen sprinkled out along the mile or so of pebbly shore, but still . . . *people.* 'We were just looking at the fossils!'

'You were *not* just looking,' growled the man, his Scottish accent deepening. Gideon had noticed that it got much more distinct when Jem was angry or stressed. 'Don't take me for an idiot, Gideon. One more trick like that and you'll be on a helicopter back to Cumbria before you can say *Oh—what happened to my holiday?*'

'What's going on in your heads?' he demanded. He took off his baseball cap, revealing close-cropped dark hair, and adjusted the almost invisible communication device inside it. 'How long have you waited for this week? Luke—you know how much it means to your mum. And yet you try to pull a Cola stunt—for what? A chunk of rock?'

Jem paused and narrowed his dark grey eyes at them. He regarded them for some time and then let his hand drop. 'It's bad enough that I have to babysit you two for a week and pretend to be your uncle,' he muttered. 'I didn't expect to have to discipline you as well.'

'You won't have to—not again!' said Gideon. 'We'll be good—perfect!'

Jem let a hint of a smile touch his mouth. 'Well—*that* wouldn't be normal and teenage would it?'

'Come on, the others are getting twitchy. Let's go and get some ice cream.' Jem turned round and headed across the beach towards a young couple who were stretched out on some beach mats. He didn't stop at their beach camp though, but just walked on along to the foot of the zigzagging cliff path, where some enterprising Islanders had set up an ice cream kiosk and a burger and hot dog stand.

Jem bought them some cones topped with a mound of fluffy white Island ice cream, each planted with a chocolate flake. They moved to a bench halfway up the cliff path to eat them, gazing back down to the beach with its sprinkling of people, brightly coloured towels, and wind breaks. Two old ladies were in fold-out chairs not far from the ice cream kiosk. The young couple they'd passed were packing up their beach mats and getting ready to go. Several bold swimmers were up to their waists in the chilly June surf. A girl with a dog was exploring one of the outcrops of pale chalky cliff face, digging at it with something and putting her finds in a battered satchel bag hanging over her shoulder. The dog—a wiry little black thing—ran up and down the slope of the crumbled cliff footings.

Her shorts and T-shirt were grubby with chalk and clay and she had some kind of ankle boots on; battered brown things with rugged soles. She did not look like a day tripper. Her limbs were lean and golden brown from regular days outdoors and she seemed entirely at ease with her task. Completely focused even when she was absent-mindedly ruffling her dog's head with one hand.

Gideon decided he fancied her. He nudged Luke and pointed down, waggling his eyebrows for effect. Luke looked and then smiled and moved his hands descriptively.

'Yup,' said Gideon. 'Definitely a bit of a babe. A rock chick. Geddit?'

Luke laughed silently.

And that was when Gideon first noticed the crack at the top of the cliff.

Three seconds later the cliff began to fall.